**'There just are times when I find it hard to keep my hands off** 

'Ditto,' she agreed, noticing the flash of desire in Zac's eyes again. 'Inner strength. We both need to find some.'

He chuckled without humour. 'It won't be easy.'

'It won't, but, nevertheless, we're two professionals who work well together and should be able to deal with seeing each other socially—'

'Without succumbing to the temptation to be in each other's arms,' he finished.

Their gazes locked, sending underlying messages of suppressed passion. Zac cleared his throat and looked away.

'I'm sorry I kissed you, Julia. I do like you, but we can only be friends. Happy families aren't for me. I won't go through it again.'

Julia frowned. *'Again?'* she whispered. What was he talking about?

**Lucy Clark** began writing romance in her early teens and immediately knew she'd found her 'calling' in life. After working as a secretary in a busy teaching hospital, she turned her hand to writing Medical Romance™. She currently lives in South Australia with her husband and two children. Lucy largely credits her writing success to the support of her husband, family and friends.

You can visit Lucy's website at www.lucyclark.net or e-mail her at lucyclark@optusnet.com.au.

**Recent titles by the same author:**

THE DOCTOR'S DILEMMA
THE SURGEON'S SECRET
THE CONSULTANT'S CONFLICT

# THE FAMILY HE NEEDS

BY
LUCY CLARK

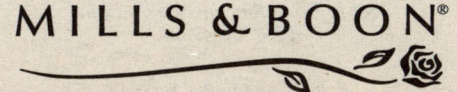

To Ellen—Thanks for loving my heroes!
Ps 90:1

**DID YOU PURCHASE THIS BOOK WITHOUT A COVER?**

If you did, you should be aware it is **stolen property** as it was reported *unsold and destroyed* by a retailer. Neither the author nor the publisher has received any payment for this book.

*All the characters in this book have no existence outside the imagination of the author, and have no relation whatsoever to anyone bearing the same name or names. They are not even distantly inspired by any individual known or unknown to the author, and all the incidents are pure invention.*

*All Rights Reserved including the right of reproduction in whole or in part in any form. This edition is published by arrangement with Harlequin Enterprises II B.V. The text of this publication or any part thereof may not be reproduced or transmitted in any form or by any means, electronic or mechanical, including photocopying, recording, storage in an information retrieval system, or otherwise, without the written permission of the publisher.*

*This book is sold subject to the condition that it shall not, by way of trade or otherwise, be lent, resold, hired out or otherwise circulated without the prior consent of the publisher in any form of binding or cover other than that in which it is published and without a similar condition including this condition being imposed on the subsequent purchaser.*

*MILLS & BOON and MILLS & BOON with the Rose Device are registered trademarks of the publisher.*

*First published in Great Britain 2002
Harlequin Mills & Boon Limited,
Eton House, 18-24 Paradise Road, Richmond, Surrey TW9 1SR*

© Lucy Clark 2002

ISBN 0 263 83056 X

*Set in Times Roman 10½ on 12 pt.
03-0302-49335*

*Printed and bound in Spain
by Litografia Rosés, S.A., Barcelona*

# CHAPTER ONE

'WHY did I let you talk me into this, Jeffrey?' Julia Bolton asked with disbelief. She looked from her position in the back seat of the Mercedes at the rear-view mirror where her gaze met Jeffrey's.

'The question you should be asking yourself is *how* you let me talk you into this,' he clarified, and his wife, who was sitting beside him, chuckled.

'He's right, Julia. My Jeffrey always is,' Mona said lovingly.

'Ah, yes, the great Dr Jeffrey McArthur. He *can* do no wrong,' Julia said with mock pride.

'I did the right thing by hiring you, Julia. You're just what the orthopaedic department needs to shake it up.'

'I don't want to shake anything up, Jeffrey. I simply want to settle into my new life here on the beautiful Gold Coast and do my job.'

'Well, you're going to shake...*something* up tonight. This guy is perfect for you.'

Julia groaned as nervous knots continued to tie themselves in her stomach.

'Relax,' Jeffrey said. 'I've known you for the past six years and I've seen what your taste in men is like.'

'Oh, so just because you didn't like my ex-husband, that means you're going to take on the role of Cupid?' Julia was amused. 'At least tell me what his name is,' she begged.

'Now, if I did that, it wouldn't be a *real* blind date,' Jeffrey said as he turned into a car park. 'We're here.

Spardo's, the best restaurant on the Gold Coast. Now, Julia,' he said as he turned to face her, 'I want you to relax and have a good time. Don't think about work or the unpacking you still have to do or even how your mother and Edward are doing. Tonight you are not a single mother who's about to start a new job on Monday. Tonight, there is only Julia—a beautiful and single woman—to be concerned with—oh, and your date, of course.'

'Of course.' She took a deep breath before getting out of the car. After her disaster of a marriage, she'd been cautious of dating. 'In for a penny...' she quoted as they all walked up the front steps of the restaurant. Her nervousness grew and she fidgeted with a shoestring strap of her mid-thigh-length black dress. Simple and elegant. Her shoulder-length dark brown curls had been hastily arranged on the top of her head with a few tendrils swirling down around her neck. Diamond stud earrings were the only jewellery she wore and her bag was clutched tightly in her right hand.

'Relax,' Mona whispered to her. She looked divine, as always. Dressed in burgundy silk with her short copper hair styled by a professional, Mona McArthur was the perfect picture of an executive's wife.

'There he is,' Jeffrey said, and Julia turned away from the direction in which he was waving.

Her heart was pounding so fiercely against her ribs she was sure everyone in the room could hear it. Why had she agreed to come? What if the night was a disaster? What if it was a success and she actually liked the man? Her mouth went dry and she swallowed a few times.

'Just breathe,' she whispered to herself, and took a deep breath. She transferred her bag to her left hand so her right was free to shake her date's hand in greeting. 'You can do this,' she said as she heard Jeffrey welcoming the man.

With a smile pasted in place, she turned around to greet her date.

When she saw who it was, she nearly fainted on the spot. Her brown eyes widened in disbelief and the smile slipped from her face, to be replaced by an open-mouthed stare. As Jeffrey continued to make the introductions, Julia's heart turned over with delight.

'Julia Bolton, meet Zachary Carmichael—ahh...but then you two already know each other,' Jeffrey said with a laugh.

Standing before her was the man of her dreams. Tall, dark and handsome. She forced her sluggish brain into action and held out her hand to him. 'Zac!' As she breathed his name the last twelve years seemed to slip away. She knew everything about this man—how he smiled, how he laughed, how he *kissed*.

'Julia.' His gaze radiated surprise as he placed his hand firmly in hers. The warmth of his touch sent a mass of tingles up her arm and she shivered with excitement. They both drank their fill of each other, their gazes locked with suppressed memories.

He hadn't changed one bit and he was still able to make her knees go weak with just one look. He took a step towards her and tugged her closer until they were only a hair's breadth apart. Neither of them spoke. Part of Julia wanted him to crush her lips to his whilst the other part wanted to slap him across the face for the pain and hurt he'd caused in the past.

She was astonished that she still had such volatile emotions as far as Zac was concerned, positive that she'd worked through these emotions a long time ago. Then again, this was the first time she'd seen him since that long-ago day when she'd walked out of his life for ever.

She angled her head, bringing it closer to his lips before

pulling back slightly. Should she kiss him? Her breathing had increased so rapidly that she was starting to become light-headed. Zac took the decision out of her hands as he pressed his lips firmly over hers.

Her eyes fluttered closed as she absorbed the magnetism of the man. If she'd thought her heart had been beating fast before, it was absolutely nothing compared to now.

A multitude of emotions raged war within her. Desire exploded throughout her body and soul as well as anger. She breathed in and the scent of his cologne assaulted her senses as his lips coaxed her mouth to open a fraction more. Every nerve ending within her body was on the alert, caught up in the sensual embrace. There was pleasure, pain and pent-up passion weaving its way around them, taking them back to a time long ago when they'd frequently been in each other's arms.

As abruptly as the kiss had begun, so it ended. Zac dropped her hand and took two steps back. Julia's breathing was as ragged as his own as they stared at each other once more. 'You look...*good*,' he said with a nod. Jeffrey's voice broke through the haze.

'I take it you two know each other?' he said.

The reality of the situation hit Julia with full force. They were standing in the foyer of the restaurant! People were staring at them! What had she been thinking?

She hadn't, she reflected, as she raised a shaky hand to lightly touch her hair. Her eyes radiated embarrassment and she glanced quickly over at Mona, who was smiling brightly.

'Jeffrey's always right,' she said softly as she looped her arm through Julia's. 'Excuse us, gentlemen,' she said in a normal tone. 'We're just going to the ladies' room to...powder our noses.'

With that, Mona whisked Julia away from the prying eyes of the other guests.

'So...tell me,' Mona encouraged as she propelled Julia into the almost vacant ladies' room. 'That wasn't a normal hello-nice-to-meet-you kiss.'

'Ah...' Julia cleared her throat. 'We used to...um... date. We dated in med school.'

'And you let him get away? Shame on you, darling,' Mona said with a delighted laugh.

Julia looked at her reflection in the mirror. She gasped when she saw the suppressed passion in her eyes, the flush of her cheeks and the parted lips that hadn't tingled like this since...well, since the last time Zac Carmichael had kissed her.

'So what happened? You can't just leave me in suspense.'

Julia shrugged. 'He moved to Sydney and I still had two years of med school to complete. I was good friends with his sister and we all stayed in contact for a few years, but it just...I don't know...dwindled, I guess.' Julia couldn't meet Mona's eyes. Zac had hurt her, humiliated her, and now here he was, back in her life. Thank goodness it was just for tonight. Hopefully she'd never run into him again and if she did, she'd be polite yet indifferent.

'Dwindled?'

'Circumstantial. He was working in one place, I was in another. Then when I moved to Western Australia, we were on opposite sides of the country.' She shook her head, trying to remove the regret from her tone. 'Australia is a big country. We just...lost contact.'

'I think there's more to it than that, Julia. I know that blasé attitude of yours, darling, and it won't wash. What *really* happened between the two of you?'

Julia looked at her reflection in the mirror before her

gaze met Mona's. She took a deep breath and said with a rush, 'We wanted different things. Zac declared that he never wanted to settle down, get married or have a family.'

'You were both young and in medical school.'

'Oh, I know that,' Julia said with an emphatic nod, the hurt and anger evident in her tone. 'But Zac said that although he quite *liked* children, he just preferred them to belong to someone else. *I* wasn't ready to start a family back then, but if I was going to transfer to a hospital close to him in Sydney and make our relationship more permanent, I needed to know whether he'd eventually change his mind.'

'And he wouldn't,' Mona said softly.

'You've got that straight.'

'He hurt you, didn't he,' Mona asked rhetorically. 'You poor thing.'

'We were so perfect together yet Zac couldn't see it. I still doubt if he can. Just because his parents had a rocky marriage, he's been afraid of commitment ever since. *Nothing* I said to him persuaded him to change his mind and in the end I got sick of trying.' There was bitterness in Julia's tone and she hung her head in regret. 'You'd think after all of these years I'd be over him,' she whispered, more to herself than to her friend.

'So what now?'

'Now?' Julia forced herself to stand tall, throwing her shoulders back. 'There's nothing now. I'm going to go out there, have dinner and go home, hoping that I never have to see Zac Carmichael again.'

Mona shook her head. 'I told Jeffrey to tell you but he wanted it to be a surprise.'

Julia's senses were once again on alert. 'What?' she asked warily.

Mona placed her hand on Julia's arm. 'Zac's your new orthopaedic colleague.'

*'What?'* Julia shook her head in disbelief. 'This isn't happening to me. It just isn't happening,' she said slowly, her eyes wide with terror. She thought about things for a moment, wondering if she could plead a headache and leave. Then again, she'd just have to face Zac again at work on Monday and then every other day for the rest of this year!

'What am I going to do?' she asked Mona.

'Perhaps Zac has changed? Perhaps he now wants to settle down and get married?'

'I doubt that. Zac's far too stubborn to change his mind. He would have to know that we're going to be working together.'

'Yes, I believe he does but he didn't know you were going to be his date for this evening. When Jeffrey suggested you as a candidate for the job, Zac's reaction was enthusiastic, to say the least. That's when my darling husband came up with the idea of setting you two up.'

'So he doesn't know about Edward?'

'Not that I know of. Jeffrey is of the opinion that you've lived your life as a single mother for the past three years and now things are going to change.'

Julia forced a smile. 'It doesn't matter what I do, Mona, I'll always be a single mother. I can go out to dinner once in a while and pretend, but the reality is I have a three-year-old son. Besides, I'm not really into trusting men all that much. After Ian's constant deceptions—'

'But Zac *isn't* Ian,' Mona interrupted. 'You can't compare every man with your ex-husband.'

'True.'

'Maybe, after time passes, you'll be able to bring yourself to trust Zac again.'

Julia sighed. 'He *was* always honest and upfront. That was one of the qualities I admired about him. He didn't beat about the bush and promise me love songs and roses when he knew it would probably never happen.'

'From the few years that we've known him, I've always found him honest, too.' Mona hesitated before saying, 'You have to admit that the attraction is still there. That kiss was testimony to it.'

Julia groaned and buried her face in her hands. 'I can't believe we just...*kissed* like that.'

'The sparks are obviously still strong between the two of you, Julia. Maybe Zac has changed. Maybe it's worth seeing if this might lead somewhere.'

Julia lifted her head, shaking it instantly. 'No. Too many hurts, too much water under the bridge.' She opened her bag and took out her deep red lipstick, raising it to her lips. It was then that she realised her hand was shaking slightly.

'Here.' Mona took the lipstick from Julia and applied it to her friend's lips. 'You're *still* affected by him, regardless of how much you'd like to deny it.' She capped the lipstick and handed it back to Julia. 'Perhaps now is the right time to take second chances. You're both ten years older and ten years wiser. Besides, after everything you've been through with Ian, you owe it to yourself to find happiness.'

'Ha! With a man who doesn't want a family?'

'Times change, people change,' Mona returned.

'You're persistent and I think you're overreacting, Mona.' Julia's tone softened as she looked at her friend. 'I know you mean well and you just want me to be as happy with someone as you are with Jeffrey.'

Mona nodded.

'We'd better get back.' Julia was glad to see her legs

had lost their wobble and seemed prepared to support her again.

'You're right. Let's get this *blind* date back on track.' As they walked out, Mona's arm linked once more with Julia's, she whispered, 'At least you have to hand it to Jeffrey. He *knew* you'd like Zac—and he was right!'

Julia laughed. 'As always.' She spied Zac first, leaning against the bar, enjoying a pre-dinner drink with Jeffrey. He must have felt her gaze because he instantly turned his head in their direction, and even from across the room Julia could read the desire smouldering in his eyes. Oh, yes, the chemistry was definitely still there.

'Ah, there you are,' Jeffrey said as his wife let go of Julia's arm and crossed to his side. 'Our table is ready. Shall we?' He offered Mona his arm and together they headed off, leaving Julia and Zac to follow suit.

'That's an amazing dress,' Zac said as Julia slipped her hand into the crook of his arm. The nearness of his body, the warmth of his touch and the way he bent slightly in her direction to speak didn't help her resolve to keep control of her emotions.

'Thank you.'

'Did you make it?'

She smiled up at him surprised that he'd remembered she'd liked to sew. 'No. Not this time. Things have been...sort of hectic...with the move and all.'

'Of course.' He nodded, then paused, before saying, 'I'm still trying to figure out *how* Jeffrey managed to talk me into this blind date, but all I can say now is I'm glad he did.'

'Really,' she said as though she didn't quite believe him. 'At least you knew we were going to be working together for the rest of the year. Jeffrey withheld that piece of information from me.'

'When did you find out?' Zac asked as they arrived at their table. He held her chair while she sat, before sitting down next to her. As he shifted his chair, Julia noticed that he also moved it slightly closer.

'About two minutes ago. Mona told me.'

'I see,' he said slowly. 'I guess that explains why you're so tense.'

During dinner, Julia ensured that they stuck to 'safe' topics of conversation rather than trying to rehash old memories. She discovered that Mona and Jeffrey had known Zac for two years. Jeffrey had left Perth General Hospital, where both he and Julia had worked, to take up the position as hospital director here on the Gold Coast. Then when the orthopaedic job had become vacant, Jeffrey had insisted Julia apply for it.

It had all happened very quickly and as she'd been hesitant about signing on with Perth General for another twelve months, she'd decided to take Jeffrey up on his offer. It had meant packing up and moving not only her son but her mother as well in just three short weeks. Nevertheless, it was all done now and on Monday she would start her new job. Alongside Zac. The thought made her uneasy. They'd never worked together as qualified surgeons before so it would be interesting to see who could be the most stubborn!

During dinner, she asked about his sister Vanessa.

'She'll be thrilled to know you're back East. She's tried on several occasions to track you down but with no success. Unfortunately, she and her family are away overseas for the next two weeks, but when she gets back we must go to Brisbane to see her.'

'Must we?' He was already making decisions for her. The instant the thought entered her head, she rejected it. Zac had never pushed her into anything, situation or otherwise, that she didn't want to do. It had been Ian who had wanted to take away her independence and she'd vowed that never again would she ever let a man have control over her mind. She would dearly love to catch up with Vanessa but whether or not she did it with Zac would need to be seen.

'It'll be just like old times,' he said, and smiled his winning smile at her. Julia smiled back politely and looked away, trying not to succumb to his natural charm. Later, as they were served coffee, she said, 'So, tell me about the orthopaedic department.'

'No.' Jeffrey held up his hand. 'No shop-talk tonight. We'll have plenty of time for that on Monday morning. This is supposed to be a *date*,' he said. 'And a very good one at that, if I do say so myself.' He grinned at them all and Mona leaned over and kissed his cheek.

'You're always right, my dear,' she said.

'I wish you'd stop telling him that, Mona,' Zac said, a teasing note in his tone. 'It makes Jeffrey think he can boss us all around at the hospital.'

Mona laughed. 'Well, he can, Zac, dear. He's the director.'

'That he may be, but telling him he's always right gives him an awfully big ego so that when he makes a mistake—'

'*If,*' Jeffrey corrected quickly, a smile on his face.

'*When,*' Julia and Zac said in unison, before laughing.

'When he makes a mistake,' Zac continued, 'it makes him unbearable to work with!'

'Well said,' Julia agreed, and they all laughed. She could feel herself slipping back into the past, enjoying his company when she really didn't want to. Typical Zac. Even when she'd been mad, he'd still been able to raise a smile from her.

When it was time to leave, they all walked out to the car park together. It was almost eleven o'clock and she was surprised at how fast the evening had gone, especially when she'd initially been thinking of ways to escape early.

'I'll take Julia home,' Zac told Jeffrey and Mona.

'Ah, that's not necessary,' she replied quickly. 'I can take a taxi. I don't want to impose,' she clarified.

'Nonsense,' Jeffrey said with a frown. 'It's no imposition. Right, Zac?'

'None at all.'

'It's all settled, then.'

Julia reluctantly agreed, not wanting to make more of a scene than she already was. 'Thank you for a lovely evening.' Julia kissed both Jeffrey and Mona goodnight.

'Give Edward a kiss from me,' Mona said softly, and Julia tensed slightly, wondering whether Zac had heard or not. She drew back from Mona and looked up at him. He was shaking hands with Jeffrey and laughing, so she presumed he hadn't heard.

'See you on Monday,' Jeffrey said, before ushering his wife to their car.

'I'm parked over here,' Zac said as he motioned to a deep green Jaguar XK8. He held the door open for Julia and waited until she was seated before walking around to the driver's side. His stride was confident, another thing that hadn't changed. Had anything? Sure, there were a few distinguished grey hairs at his temple, but externally he was exactly as she remembered. Was Mona right? Had his opinions changed over time?

The car itself, with its two doors and soft top, declared he was a single man who liked to live life in the fast lane. That's how he'd been in med school and she wondered whether Zac still held to the opinion of never having a family.

He turned and smiled at her and she brushed the thoughts away, intent, for the moment, on just enjoying his company. 'Would you like me to take the top off the car? You know, cruise along, enjoying the warm January breeze?'

Julia shook her head. 'It's me, Zac. You don't need to impress me with your fancy sports car.' She leaned a little closer and whispered, 'I know you, remember.' Her gaze flicked from his eyes to his lips, the sensual moment enveloping them both. 'I know the *real* Zachary Carmichael.'

'Promise me you won't tell anyone,' he joked. He started the engine as they both pulled their seat belts on. 'So, tell me about your life, Jules. What have you been doing for the past decade?'

It had been a long time since anyone had called her Jules and she felt pleasure at hearing it again. When she didn't say anything, he asked, 'Where do you live?'

She told him and he turned the car in that direction. 'Nice and close to the hospital,' he said, and she nodded.

'Mona chose the house mainly for its location.'

'You've known them for a while?'

'About six years. Jeffrey and I worked at the same hospital in Perth for several years. It was through him that I met my ex-husband.'

'So you did get married.' He nodded as though he'd expected it. 'Sorry it didn't work out.'

'At least say it like you mean it.'

'So what happened?' The question was asked lightly.

'I guess it was the tiny fact that he thought he could sleep with whomever he wanted while I thought the two of us should be exclusive. After all, we *were* married.'

'I see.' The words were spoken slowly as though he was putting his own interpretation on it.

'What do you see?' she asked him, deciding to take the bull by the horns.

He glanced over at her and then back to the road. 'That you're probably not too good at trusting men any more.'

Julia laughed without humour. 'Nope. Not too good at trusting them at all,' she agreed. 'Jeffrey and Mona were a great support and helped me through the divorce.'

'They are a great couple and perfectly matched.' He stopped at a red light and turned to face her. 'I *am* sorry you've been hurt,' he said with sincerity.

She willed herself to be strong and not fall for the tenderness he was offering. 'Yeah, well, I'm finally starting to see a pattern. I seem to be attracted to men who can't commit. You were honest but were afraid of commitment and while Ian was happy to commit, he wasn't too honest.'

Their gazes held and Zac brought his hand up to caress her face, his thumb gently rubbing over her mouth. 'I'm sorry,' he said tenderly. 'I'm so sorry I hurt you.'

Julia was mesmerised by him but forced herself to pull back. He dropped his hand. 'Yeah, well...I got over it.'

The blaring of a car horn behind them snapped them back to reality and they both turned to see that the light was now green.

Zac set the Jag in motion and just as they crossed the intersection the light turned amber again. 'So...' He cleared his throat. 'There's no special...man in your life right now?'

Julia frowned and hesitated. *Had* he heard Mona telling her to kiss Edward? His mobile phone shrilled to life, saving her from answering. He quickly pulled over to the side of the road and answered the call.

'Dr Carmichael,' he said into the receiver. He paused for a moment. 'Where?' Another pause. 'We'll be right there.' He disconnected the call and looked over his shoulder to check the traffic before indicating and turning the car around.

'Problem?'

'That was Jeffrey. MVA at a major intersection not far from the restaurant we were at tonight. A minibus full of tourists crashed with a semi-trailer. Jeffrey's called the police and ambulance and together with Mona, they're trying to organise things.' Zac increased his speed slightly, watching the traffic carefully. He was a good, safe driver and she was thankful that that hadn't changed.

Within five minutes, they were passing the restaurant and he continued onwards. Soon the traffic started to bank up because of the accident. Zac pulled off the road and parked the car half on the kerb. Next he switched on his hazard lights and cut the engine. They both climbed from the car at the same time, Zac only stopping to collect his medical bag.

'At least with Jeffrey in charge, things should be well organised,' Zac mumbled as they covered the remaining distance to the accident site.

'He can also lend a hand. He may have gone into administration but he's still a qualified medical doctor,' she added. 'It might even give us a chance to boss *him* around for a change,' Julia said, and Zac turned to smile quickly at her.

'Yes. Maybe *we* can be right for a change!'

## CHAPTER TWO

'STATUS?' Zac asked as they crossed to where Jeffrey was kneeling by a man who was lying on the ground. Zac opened his bag and handed Julia a pair of gloves, before pulling on a pair himself.

Julia looked up for a moment to where Mona was surrounded by a few people, all talking to her at once. All were Japanese tourists and in their early to mid-twenties. It was then that Julia recalled that Mona spoke the language. What a stroke of luck!

'He went through the windscreen of the minibus,' Jeffrey stated as he moved away so that Julia and Zac had more room. Zac knelt beside the patient and introduced himself.

'I'm Zac and this is Julia,' he stated, but the man had a vacant look in his eyes as though he didn't understand a word Zac was saying.

'Check him out,' he told Julia. 'Can we get a translator over here?' he asked Jeffrey.

'I'll get Mona.' Jeffrey nodded.

Julia checked the patient's vital signs. 'Stable,' she reported to Zac. Next she ran her hands over his body, checking for fractures. 'From what I can tell, he's dislocated his right shoulder and fractured his left tibia. Right wrist also doesn't look too good. Facial lacerations,' Julia murmured as she carefully checked around his skull.

'Mona's on her way,' Jeffrey said when he returned. 'This guy's the worst of the lot and, as you can hear, his breathing is very raspy as well.'

'Asthmatic?' Julia asked.

Jeffrey nodded. 'Mona's spoken to the driver.' He pointed to a man sitting on the side of the road, his head buried in his hands. 'He said this guy here was wheezing and starting to panic. He was heading for the hospital when the accident occurred.'

'We'll have to keep a close eye on him,' Zac said as he, too, checked the patient out for fractures. 'You're all right,' he soothed, seeing the terror and uncertainty in the man's eyes. 'Right femur doesn't feel too good either. Julia, there's some saline in my bag. Let's get an IV set up and stabilise him while we wait for the ambulance.'

'What's the ambulance's ETA?' Julia asked Jeffrey.

'I called them before I called you, so hopefully soon.'

'I'm here,' Mona said, her tone holding a thread of weariness. She crouched down beside Zac.

'Patient's name?'

Mona spoke in Japanese and Julia noticed how the patient relaxed a little. 'Ishimaru,' she told them. 'Aki Ishimaru.'

'Good. Let him know that we're doctors and we're waiting for the ambulance.' Zac waited while Mona spoke. 'Confirm that he's asthmatic, please.'

*'Zensokuga arimaska.'*

Aki nodded sadly before closing his eyes and whispering, *'Zensokuga arimaska.'*

Mona gave him a concerned look before she looked to Julia and Zac, 'Yes, he does have asthma,' she confirmed.

'OK. We're going to give him something for the pain now. Does he have any allergies?'

Mona spoke again and then translated. 'He's not allergic to anything.'

Zac nodded as he drew up an injection of morphine.

'We'll need to monitor his asthma closely,' he murmured to Julia, who agreed.

Zac explained how they needed to stabilise Aki's femur and had Mona translate. 'If that's all for the moment,' Mona said as she stood again, 'I can hear someone calling for me.'

'Thanks,' Zac said. 'Jeffrey, you check out the other patients while we stabilise this man. Scissors,' he said to Julia, as Jeffrey left them to it. Julia dug around in his medical bag and pulled out a pair of heavy-duty scissors. Zac cut through the man's denim jeans to allow access to the injury on the right thigh while Julia continued setting up an IV line. The femur was their top priority as their patient could quite easily bleed to death from such an injury.

Julia inserted the cannula into the man's left arm, then made sure the saline was dripping at the correct rate before performing the neurological and neurovascular observations again.

'This femur is a mess,' Zac said after he'd revealed the wound. 'We need to get him stabilised before he loses any more blood.'

They worked methodically together and just before they were finished Jeffrey came back.

'Is one of you free? Mona says another patient has just lost consciousness. She apparently hit her head quite hard on a window when they crashed.'

'We're almost done,' Zac murmured. 'Julia, you take the other patient. I'll stay here and monitor this one.' After a few more minutes, the soft-tissue damage was stabilised and Julia could go.

Jeffrey led her over to where the woman had lost consciousness in the middle of the road. Traffic was still heavily banked up and some motorists had volunteered to redirect the cars until the police could get through.

Julia heard the wail of sirens in the distance and was thankful that help had finally arrived. Zac only had limited emergency supplies in his bag and she hadn't thought to bring her own. After all, she was supposed to be on a date!

'Can you hear me?' Julia said as she crouched down beside the woman. 'Has she lost consciousness before?'

'Not that I'm aware of.' Jeffrey looked at the woman's friend and asked him, but he just shook his head and shrugged.

'Get Mona to translate and double-check,' Julia requested. She checked the woman's pupils with Zac's medical torch and was pleased to note they were equal and reacting to light. She continued to perform the observations, and when she'd finished she looked up at Jeffrey.

'Pulse rate and breathing are both slightly rapid but nothing to be concerned with at the moment. Her hands are a bit clammy but that's to be expected. I'd say concussion but we'll need to watch she doesn't go into shock. I'd like her to have a skull X-ray when she gets to Emergency.'

Mona came over at Jeffrey's urging. She looked exhausted, Julia thought, but knew her friend would be fine when this ordeal was over. Mona asked the woman's friend the question and Julia was relieved when the young man shook his head quite emphatically.

'Good.' Julia took the woman's pulse again.

'Wait a minute,' Mona said as the man started talking again. 'He said she vomited just before she fainted.'

Julia nodded. 'That's normal with concussion. Can you hear me?' she called, and the woman started to rouse. Her eyelids fluttered open momentarily. 'Do you remember where you are?' Julia asked, but the woman didn't understand. Before she could ask, Mona had translated and told Julia that the woman remembered the bus crash.

'Need a hand?' another voice said from behind her, and she turned to see a woman in a paramedic's uniform.

'Most *definitely*.' Julia was thankful help was finally there. 'Can you check her blood pressure for me, please, and watch for signs of delayed shock? Otherwise, at this stage, treat her for concussion.'

'Sure thing.' The paramedic crouched down beside the patient and fitted a portable sphygmomanometer around the patient's arm and checked her blood pressure.

'Julia!'

The urgency in Zac's tone alerted her and she hurried to his side.

'His breathing is worse.' Zac turned to address the paramedic who had just set up a unit of blood to transfuse the patient. 'I need oxygen—eight litres—and a bronchodilator through a nebuliser mask.'

The paramedic nodded before sprinting back to the parked ambulance.

'Help me lift him up,' Zac said to Julia, and together they elevated their patient. When they had him elevated, he said, 'I'll hold him, you do his obs. It's all right, Aki. Deep breaths,' Zac encouraged.

Julia monitored Aki's respiration rate and took his pulse. The paramedic returned with the oxygen and bronchodilator as well as an oximeter and portable sphygmo.

Julia finished listening to the man's chest, not liking what she'd heard. 'Very moist in those lungs. The left lobe sounds worse than the right,' she informed Zac. 'Let's get the oxygen going and get an oximeter reading.'

They waited for a few seconds. 'Oxygen saturation is eighty-five per cent with oxygen running. We need to start the bronchodilator medication,' Zac commented.

'Can you hear me?' Julia called to Aki, and slowly his eyelids fluttered open but only for a moment before they closed again. 'This is a bronchodilator drug,' Julia told the patient. 'This will help relax the muscles in your lungs. You need to breathe deeply,' she tried to encourage. They fitted the mask over his mouth and nose. 'Deep breaths,' Julia encouraged as she, too, took a deep breath.

Aki sucked in a raspy breath but at least he knew what to do.

'Let's get Aki ready to transfer,' Zac said a few moments later. 'The sooner he's on his way to hospital, the better.'

As they were getting him into the ambulance, another one arrived. Julia went across to speak to Jeffrey while Zac gave a quick hand-over to the other paramedics. 'Zac and I are going to take Aki to the hospital.' She pointed to the ambulance where the patient was safely ensconced.

Mona came up behind her husband. 'Whew! I'm exhausted but, still, there's work to do. You off to Theatre with Aki now?'

'Yes,' Julia replied, and touched her friend's arm. 'Take a deep breath. You'll do fine.'

'Off you go,' Jeffrey said with a nod in the direction of the ambulance.

As the ambulance navigated its way through the banked-up traffic, which the police were now controlling, Zac and Julia kept a close eye on Aki's condition. Although his breath was rasping, the airways were still clear and the bronchodilator was working.

When they arrived at Gold Coast General, Zac wrote out a list of X-rays and tests needed before handing Aki over to the accident and emergency crew.

'Let's head to Emergency Theatres and get the equipment ready,' he suggested to Julia. 'It'll also give me a chance to give you a quick tour. A *very* quick tour.' He smiled at her and Julia's heart rate increased. She returned his smile and walked beside him as he headed off down a pale green corridor.

'In here,' he said, opening a door, 'is the family waiting room.'

Julia saw some comfortable chairs as well as tea and coffee facilities. There were magazines on the table—the basics but, then, what did people want while they were waiting for their loved ones to come out of surgery?

'Further down here,' he said as they went through some swinging doors into an area marked STAFF ONLY, 'is the doctors' tearoom.' Zac rounded a corner and opened the door. This room was a lot larger and had comfortable chairs as well as tables and chairs for people to work at. There was a small kitchen bench, which had tea- and coffee-making facilities and a sink for people to wash their cups up in. A few Impressionist prints were hung on the walls, as well as one large X-ray viewing box.

'That's the essentials out of the way,' he said. 'Where to find the coffee and the patient's family!' He grinned at her and raised his eyebrows. 'Well, perhaps I'll show you where we'll be operating as well.'

'Might be handy.' The laughter was evident in her tone. There were three emergency theatres, all different sizes, and after introducing Julia to Beatrice, the sister in charge, Zac organised Aki Ishimaru's operation.

They would need to debride and insert a Grosse and Kempf intramedullary nailing rod down the centre of the femur, as well as relocate the right shoulder, and that was just for starters. Once they'd had a good look at the X-rays Zac had requested, things would be clearer.

Zac directed Julia to the changing rooms and showed her where to find the scrubs. As she went in to get changed, she looked at her elegant black dress in the mirror and smiled sadly, shaking her head. 'Interesting night,' she murmured to herself.

'Most definitely,' a female voice said from behind her, and Julia looked at Beatrice's reflection in the mirror before turning around. 'Sorry,' she said quickly. 'I didn't mean to startle you.'

Julia returned the smile. 'No need to apologise. It's just been a little hectic this evening.'

'Out on a date?' Beatrice crossed to her locker.

Julia thought for a moment. She guessed it was probably wise not to tell Beatrice the whole truth about tonight, that being Jeffrey's attempt to set her and Zac up as a couple. 'Of sorts. Jeffrey McArthur wanted to introduce me to Zac. On the way home, there was an accident!'

'Ain't it just like those MVAs.' Beatrice shook her head in mock disgust.

'Too true,' Julia agreed as she started taking the pins from her hair. She shook out her curls and ran her fingers through them. 'Right now, though, I'd better get changed. I don't want to keep Zac waiting.' She pulled her hair back into a ponytail to keep it out of the way.

'Oh, sure,' Beatrice said as she returned her focus back to her locker. She took out a packet of lollies and offered one to Julia.

'No, thanks.'

'I'm trying to quit smoking,' Beatrice confided. 'These help and they're sugar-free,' she said as she munched on the lolly. 'So what do you think of GCH's most eligible bachelor?'

'Zac?' Julia's smile was completely natural. 'Zac is the most eligible bachelor? This hospital needs some new blood.'

'What? You don't think he's good-looking?' Beatrice asked in amazement. 'Are you *blind*?'

Julia laughed. 'Of course I think he's good-looking but Zac and I are old friends.' There, it was out. The hospital grapevine would be buzzing with rumours by the time Monday morning came—her official starting date.

She'd made sure she hadn't hesitated, that she'd said it as though it were nothing—common knowledge. Julia continued changing. 'His sister, Vanessa, and I were in med school together.'

'*Really!* What a small world.'

'You can say that again.' Julia laughed. She closed the locker she'd been assigned. 'Right now, though, I'd better go and find the man we're discussing and track down the patient's X-rays.'

'Yeah sure. Well, well. You already knew him.'

'Meaning?' Julia stopped by the changing room doors.

'Just when the hospital grapevine heard the new orthopod was a female, some staff started placing bets that the two of you would get together.'

'Why? Does Zac have a habit of falling for every woman he works with?'

Beatrice shrugged. 'Has been known to happen!' With that, she merely smiled and shoved another lolly in her mouth.

Julia frowned and continued on her way. What was that cryptic comment supposed to mean? Then again, did she really want to know about Zac's love life during the past ten years? At the moment, she decided, ignorance was bliss.

'Ah, there you are,' he said when she re-entered the doctors' tearoom. 'Looking exquisite in hospital green scrubs. Only you could do them such justice, Jules,' he murmured. 'Nice hairstyle, too.' He flicked her ponytail.

'Now, *this* is the Julia Bolton I remember. Scruffy-looking with ponytail in place.'

Julia smiled at him. 'Any news on the X-rays?' He was so…the *same*, and she'd always enjoyed his company.

'First lot of films are on their way here right now.'

'Good.'

Zac narrowed his gaze. 'Is everything all right?'

Julia cleared her throat and nodded. 'Sure. Everything's just…peachy.'

'Why is your surname still Bolton?' he asked quietly. 'You didn't want to take your husband's surname?'

Julia looked down at her hands before looking up at Zac. 'A lot of female doctors prefer to use their maiden name for consulting purposes,' she replied.

'You're avoiding the question. Why?'

She shrugged. 'No real secrecy. I just prefer not to talk about it. My life with Ian was…' she shook her head '…such a long time ago. I've changed a lot since then.'

'Hi, Zac,' a female voice said, and in walked a woman who Julia guessed to be five feet exactly. 'Radiology asked me to bring these to you.' She handed him a packet of X-rays.

Julia was relieved at the interruption.

'Hi,' the other woman said, holding out her hand to Julia. 'I'm Lucille Barnstock, the anaesthetist.'

'Nice to meet you,' Julia replied.

'Have you reviewed the patient?' Zac asked as he hooked the films up onto the viewing box.

'Yes. His breathing is more stable now,' Lucille reported as they all gathered around.

'Femur nailing looks as though it's going to be straightforward,' Zac mumbled as he changed the view of the fracture.

'How's his spinal column?' Julia asked, and Zac

swapped the films over. 'Let's see...' They all peered closely at the film. 'Looks OK.' He turned to face Lucille. 'I guess we're ready when you are.'

'What about the shoulder?' the anaesthetist asked.

'Good question,' Zac replied, and hunted through the packet of films. He swapped the views over.

'Nice and clean,' Julia announced. 'We can relocate that once he's under.'

'Sure,' Lucille answered. 'Well, I'd best get changed. See you both in Theatre,' she tossed over her shoulder as she left the room.

'At least his breathing has improved,' Julia remarked as she looked at the femoral views once more. 'Is Lucille good?'

'One of the best anaesthetists I've worked with,' Zac said with a nod.

'Should be no problems then.'

He was standing very close and Julia found herself holding her breath, looking unseeingly at the X-rays before her. Unbelievable! Her entire body was tuned to his every movement. How had this happened so quickly? They'd only been in each other's company for a matter of hours and it was as though the years had disappeared.

His hands came up, one on either side, to touch her arms and he bent his head close to her ear. 'You can feel it, can't you?' he whispered, causing goose-bumps to spread over her body. 'It's as though we've never been apart.'

Julia closed her eyes and took a steadying breath, trying to calm her senses. Instead, the scent of his cologne wound its way around her, making her feel light-headed and helpless.

'Zachary,' she whispered as he slowly turned her to face him. She opened her eyes and looked up, still feeling as though she were dreaming.

'This is...'

'Uncanny,' she finished for him with a nod. 'I know, and it feels so...'

'Right.' He looked down at her for a few more seconds before taking a step back. He turned and looked at a picture on the wall moments before the door opened and Beatrice came in. Julia turned around, unable to look the nurse in the face.

'Here are the rest of Aki Ishimaru's X-rays.'

'Thanks.' Zac nodded and returned to Julia's side at the viewing box. 'Let's have a look at these.' He hooked up the views of the wrist fracture first and then the left tibial fracture.

'Both quite clean,' Julia said with a nod. 'Plaster of Paris ought to do the trick.'

'Agreed.' Zac gathered up all of the radiographs and put them in the packet. 'Let's go see how Aki is coping.' His tone was professional and so was the way he turned and walked out of the room.

'Professional,' she reminded herself. She was here because she had a job to do, not because she wanted to reignite the sparks that appeared so naturally between herself and Zac.

They checked on Aki who was now drowsy from his pre-med, although still able to mutter, '*Taskete. Taskete kudasai.*'

'What?' Zac asked, looking around at one of the nursing staff.

'It means, "Help. Help, please,"' Beatrice translated. She spoke to him in his native tongue and within a few minutes Aki was once again reassured and resting comfortably.

He was wheeled into Theatre and into Lucille's care.

'We'll relocate his shoulder and then tackle the intramedullary nailing of the femur,' Zac advised. It was clear who was the senior surgeon. Julia nodded as they made their way to the scrub sink.

'Once we're done there, we'll apply POP to the right wrist and left tibia. Then hopefully—' his voice dropped to a more quiet tone '—we can finish our date and I can take you home!'

Julia smiled up at him but was saved the trouble of replying when the scrub nurse came to help them. The operation went well and the procedure of stabilising the femoral shaft with a G&K intramedullary nail was completed without complication.

Julia had been a little bit anxious about operating with Zac as they'd never worked together in such an anticipatory role before. As it turned out, she'd had nothing to fear as they'd complemented each other to perfection.

After Aki stabilised and had left Recovery for the critical care unit, Julia went back to the changing rooms, feeling a little ridiculous as she changed back into her little black dress.

There was no way she'd be able to get her hair back into the style that she'd worn earlier. That had required her mother's assistance, and as it was now almost time for the sun to rise Julia couldn't be bothered.

She smothered a yawn as she pulled her hair from the ponytail and fluffed her fingers through the curls. Edward would be waking up soon and demanding Mummy's attention.

She smiled at her reflection at the thought of her son. Nothing like a child to keep you humble as well as exhausted, although at this stage her new job was taking all the credit for the exhaustion part.

Glad it was now Sunday, Julia was happy she could rest and relax before starting her new job the next day. She left the changing rooms and went in search of Zac. She found him in the middle of the main corridor, talking to Beatrice, looking magnificently male in his dark suit.

'Ah, there you are, Julia. Ready?' He raised his eyebrows as his gaze skimmed quickly and appreciatively over her black dress and her long legs revealed beneath it.

At his glance her breath was momentarily caught in her throat and she found herself unable to speak, so she nodded instead.

'Good.' He turned back to Beatrice. 'Thanks for the update. Call me if there are any complications.'

'Will do,' Beatrice said. 'See you tomorrow, Julia.'

Julia cleared her throat and smiled. 'Yes.'

They walked out of the hospital together and over to Zac's car. 'So much for a nice relaxing evening,' he said as he smothered a yawn. He held the door for her before walking around to the driver's side. 'Beatrice just advised me that all the other tourists have been attended to and all kept in overnight for observation.'

'Good.'

Neither of them spoke much on the drive, except for taking it in turns to yawn.

'Stop yawning,' Julia accused lightly. 'You're making me tired.'

Zac chuckled as he turned into Julia's street, following her directions. He pulled up outside her house and cut the engine. 'Stay there. I'll get the door,' he said when she undid her seat belt. He strode around and opened her door, offering his hand to help her out.

Julia accepted and swung one high-heeled foot out before the other followed suit. She watched as Zac once more appraised her legs and she smiled.

'Perfect legs—as always,' he murmured, before closing the car door. He refused to let go of her hand as they walked up the front path. When they reached the door, they stopped and turned to face each other.

'Julia, tonight has been a revelation. The chemistry between us is still very much alive and I think we should—'

'See where it leads us?' she interrupted.

'Yes. I want to see you again.' He yawned and they both laughed.

'You will,' she said teasingly. 'We're going to be working together for the next twelve months.'

'That's not what I meant,' he said, his smile causing her to forget all rational thought. 'How about next Saturday night? Just the two of us.'

Julia thoughts turned instantly to Edward. He hadn't wanted her to go out last night and as they'd just arrived in the Gold Coast he still needed time to settle into his new environment. Edward might be used to her working all hours of the day and night, but the sooner he settled back into his previous routine, the better. It was one of the reasons her mother lived with them—to provide a stable home environment for Edward while his mother went off to work. 'I...I would need to check my roster. I might be on call next Saturday.'

'We both are,' he said. 'As we're the only two full-time orthopaedic surgeons employed at the hospital, we alternate the emergency roster during the week but we're both always on call for the weekends. Except for once a month when a locum comes down from Brisbane and we both get the weekend off.'

'So this isn't the weekend off.'

'No, but, like tonight, if there is an emergency, at least we'll still be together.'

A war raged within Julia. Should she or shouldn't she? She hadn't dated for the past three years since she'd divorced Ian. Mainly because of Edward but also because she was through dating men with hang-ups. One thing she'd rediscovered tonight had been that she liked being with Zac. They shared the same sense of humour, the same drive and ambition. And despite everything that had happened between them, she'd still had fun. 'I'll think about it,' she answered finally.

'I guess that's all I can ask.' With that, Zac took a step forward and placed his hands on her arms. 'How is it that you're more beautiful than ever?'

Julia's breath caught in her throat at the compliment. It had been a long time since a man had thought her beautiful and the sweet words bolstered her damaged ego. She forced herself to meet his gaze. 'Thank you.' The atmosphere between them grew thick with repressed tensions. 'Zac?' she whispered as his hands slid up her arms to cup her face.

'Hmm?'

'Don't hurt me again.' She closed her eyes as his head slowly descended towards her lips. He brushed them lightly across hers before looking down at her.

'I never intended to hurt you in the first place, Jules.' His words were spoken with honest sincerity. Again, he brushed his lips across hers.

Julia's eyelids fluttered closed and she sighed into the embrace as she threaded her fingers through his hair, opening her mouth to accept his kiss. This time, his lips were soft and gentle on hers, unlike the fiery greeting they'd shared back at the restaurant. His hands moved downwards, his thumbs gently grazing the sides of her breasts as he slid his arms beneath hers, enabling him to gather her closer.

He groaned and deepened the kiss, the fire and passion scorching through both of them just as it had long ago.

Zac's kisses had sweetened Julia's dreams for years and here she was again, back in his arms.

Zac was a very handsome man. Ian, too, had been tall, dark and handsome, but where Zac had morals and ethics, Ian hadn't. She'd known, back in medical school, that Zac was going to make a wonderful doctor and it was him she had to thank for her love of orthopaedics.

She'd become quite successful in the orthopaedic field herself, even though she'd been juggling motherhood and her career for the past three years. Edward! The thought of her son was enough to help her break away from the memories Zac's kisses were evoking.

Julia rested her head against his shoulder as her ragged breathing slowly returned to normal. 'Do you have any idea what you do to me?'

'Exactly the same as what *you* do to *me*,' he answered, and wrapped her securely in his arms, his own breathing slightly uneven. 'Fate has brought us together once again, Julia.'

'Don't tell Jeffrey or he'll be jealous of fate.'

Zac chuckled. 'Good point.' He kissed her briefly again. 'Aren't you going to invite me in for breakfast?' His voice was low and personal.

'Zac,' Julia warned.

He stepped back and held up his hands in defence. '*Just* breakfast,' he said with a teasing grin. 'I'm starving, Jules.'

She smiled at him but it didn't reach her eyes. She knew she had to tell him about Edward, even though she didn't want to—not yet. Julia knew Zac would retreat once he found out she was a single mother. Families and Zachary Carmichael just didn't mix. She took a deep breath, hoping amongst hope that time *had* changed him as she said softly, 'I would, Zac but...I don't live alone.'

The teasing look in his eyes disappeared immediately,

to be replaced by a serious glare. 'You said you weren't involved with anyone. I asked you straight out and you said no,' he reminded her.

'I'm not,' she mumbled as her mobile phone rang. She stopped and reached into her bag, quickly connecting the call. 'Hello,' she said after clearing her throat, watching as Zac raked one hand through his hair, the other hand in his trouser pocket.

'Julia, it's Mum. Edward's just come into my room saying that he can't find you.'

'There was an emergency. I'm outside the front door right now,' she said, still watching Zac.

'Oh! In that case, we'll be right out.'

Julia didn't reply but disconnected the call. Whether she was ready for it or not, Zac was about to meet Edward.

'Who's Edward?' Zac asked the instant Julia had ended the call and she frowned. Had he been able to read her mind? When she didn't say anything, he continued, 'I thought I heard Mona tell you to give Edward a kiss. I know Edward was your father's name and I also know that he died just before you finished med school. I went to the funeral, remember. Or did I just overhear Mona incorrectly?'

'Edward.' She nodded. 'You heard Mona correctly. Zac, Edward is my—'

She was stopped as a loud, excited shriek came from inside her house. 'Mummy! Mummy! Where my mummy?' A split second later, the front door was wrenched open and Edward hurtled himself past his grandmother, heading straight for Julia.

She bent down and scooped him up, giving him a kiss. As she straightened, she turned her gaze to meet Zac's.

He looked at her with absolute astonishment, his jaw open in disbelief.

## CHAPTER THREE

'I FOUND my mummy,' Edward squealed as he wrapped his little arms about Julia's neck.

'Zac,' Julia said, after taking a shaky breath, 'I'd like you to meet my son. Edward.'

Edward shifted in her arms to look at Zac. 'Hello. I E'ward. Wha's your name?'

'Ah...Zac,' he replied after a moment, looking from Julia to her son and back again.

'Zac Carmichael!' Cassandra said, and leaned over to kiss his cheek. 'What a surprise to see you on our doorstep.' Julia watched as her mother looked from her to Zac and back again. A smile started to spread across her face. 'Oh, don't tell me that *Zac* was your blind date last night?' She chuckled, neither Zac nor Julia saying a word. 'Did Jeffrey know? I mean, did he know that you two knew each other?'

'Uh...yes.' Julia was watching Zac carefully, still trying to gauge his reaction.

'Oh, that's just like Jeffrey.' Cassandra continued to laugh and Julia glared at her mother. 'Listen, why don't we all go inside and catch up?' Cassandra suggested. 'You two both look exhausted and in need of strong coffee.' With that, she turned and led the way.

'After you,' Julia said as Edward scrambled from her arms and ran after his grandmother. It was out in the open and now she was waiting desperately for a sign from him as to what would happen next.

'I...should go,' he mumbled, but didn't move.

There's your answer! His words pierced her heart. So much for hoping he might have changed his attitude. She crossed her arms defensively in front of her and nodded silently, unable to speak.

'The coffee's fresh,' Cassandra called from the kitchen.

Zac still hadn't moved and Julia sensed there was a war taking place deep within him. Edward came running back, holding something in his hands. She instantly recognised them as his two favourite little cars which Jeffrey had given him when they'd arrived last week.

'A special moving present,' he'd called them, and Edward hadn't left the house without his two special cars ever since.

'Look, look,' he said, and thrust the cars at Zac. 'D'are mine. D'ere E'ward's *shpeshial* cars!' His eyes were so alive with excitement at showing Zac his *special* cars that Julia couldn't resist smiling.

She looked up at Zac who appeared to still be in shock.

'Ah...nice,' he mumbled towards Edward, but didn't take the cars her son was so eagerly holding out to him.

'Toast is up,' Cassandra called, and Julia headed into the kitchen, hoping that Zac would follow.

'Tum on,' Edward urged Zac, as he followed his mother and grandmother. 'Tum on. Play with *shpeshial* cars,' he said excitedly.

Julia looked back over her shoulder to see her son tugging at Zac's trouser leg with his free hand. 'Tum *on*,' he urged again. Julia found it difficult to keep the smile off her face—Edward was just *so* cute!

Hesitantly, as though he was fighting it with everything he had, Zac allowed Edward to drag him through the house and into the kitchen.

'How do you take your coffee, Zac?' Cassandra asked as she poured three cups.

'Ah…sorry. I need to go,' he said firmly, and turned on his heel and walked out of the kitchen. Edward started to follow him but Cassandra called him back. Julia slumped down into a chair at the kitchen table and buried her face in her hands, wincing as she heard the front door shut with finality.

Zac strode down the front path and climbed into his car. He forced himself to slow down. He was in shock, as well as being fatigued from the long night at the hospital. Pushing all thoughts of Julia to the back of his mind, Zac drove the Jaguar to his apartment ten minutes away.

It was situated in one of the many high-rise apartment buildings scattered along the coastline of beautiful beaches. He promised himself a dip in the warm sea water later—after he'd caught up on some sleep.

He parked the car in his designated place and rode the lift to the nineteenth floor. After collecting his morning paper, he unlocked the door and walked in. Once a week, his apartment was cleaned and he acknowledged his own superior judgement in purchasing a place that was serviced.

Several of the apartments in the building were available for rent on a permanent or casual basis and so the building came complete with its own room service. A facility that a busy doctor like himself frequently used, such as now, he thought as he crossed to the phone and ordered breakfast.

'I'm a single man,' Zac said out loud. 'And I like it.' So why didn't the words sound as convincing as he'd hoped? He looked towards his study before shaking his head and walking into the kitchen.

Zac poured himself a glass of cold orange juice and took a sip. Glass in hand, he prowled around the apartment, trying to control his thoughts. Eventually he ended up in his study and slowly crossed to his desk. He sat down in the comfortable leather chair, old memories starting to encompass him—not of Julia but of what she represented.

He placed his glass on the desk and extended his hand to the bottom drawer. Taking a deep breath, Zac pulled it open and looked sadly down at the woman smiling back at him from the silver frame.

He took it out and sat it in the middle of his desk, forcing himself to breathe deeply. Cara's blue eyes stared laughingly back at him. She looked so well, so healthy, so happy. *They* had been happy. Maybe there hadn't been the immense spark or chemistry that flowed so naturally between Julia and himself, but he had loved Cara. Loved her enough to marry her—and now she was gone.

Zac wasn't sure how long he'd sat there but the buzz from his front door brought him out of his reverie. Carefully he replaced the photograph in the drawer before closing it—locking away the memories that played no part in his current life.

The buzzer rang again.

'Coming,' he called impatiently, and hurried to the door.

'Room service,' the attendant called. As Zac opened the door, the phone rang.

'Ugh,' he groaned, and left the waiter to set up as he hurried to the phone. 'Dr Carmichael,' he answered.

'Zac? It's Rodney.'

Great, Zac thought. His registrar was calling him—he glanced at the clock—just over an hour after he'd left the hospital. There must be a problem. Into the receiver he said, 'What's the problem, Rod?'

'Aki Ishimaru has a problem with one of the drains.'

'Get him prepped. I'm on my way.' Zac disconnected the call and looked at his breakfast. Stopping long enough to put plastic wrap on the bacon and eggs and store it in the refrigerator, he grabbed the croissant and took a few mouthfuls of the hot coffee. 'That'll have to do—for now,' he mumbled as he grabbed his keys and walked out of the door.

'Wake up, Mummy. Wake up.' Edward's little voice pierced through her dreams of Zac and Julia opened her eyes to find her son's face only millimetres from her own.

'Whoa!' she said as she drew back, momentarily shocked. Edward giggled.

'I's morning, Mummy. I's morning,' he said at the top of his lungs.

'Shh, darling. I know.' Julia shifted in the bed and made room for her son, helping him to climb onto her bed. He snuggled beside her and she closed her eyes in delight. 'Mmm, what a lovely cuddle.'

'I know, Mum. I know. Let's have a pillow pight.'

'I know, I know,' Julia replied sleepily as she held onto her son, kissing his forehead. 'Let's not have a pillow fight just yet. Mummy's still waking up.'

'Oh-tay.'

She felt Edward's arms come around her neck and he hugged her close, his little fingers tangling in her hair. She winced but didn't dare take his arms away. Cuddles like this were a precious gift from her son and she cherished every single one she received. Besides, Edward was incapable of staying still for more than three seconds together!

But *this* was what life was all about. Until she'd had Edward, she'd only been existing. 'Where's Grandma?' she asked him.

'I know, I know,' he bellowed in her ear, before scrambling from her bed. 'Tum on, Mummy. Let's find Gr'ma.'

'You go first,' she suggested as she stretched. 'I'm coming.'

'Oh-tay,' he said as he ran off at top speed.

Julia smiled. He was gorgeous. *So is Zac*, her subconscious chimed in. She breathed in deeply as the memory of his kisses returned. Zac was wonderful. Charming, good-looking, caring...the list went on and on but... She came down to earth with a thud as she remembered the way he'd left yesterday morning.

'But,' she said aloud as she swung her legs over the bed and sat upright, 'he doesn't want a family.' It was the way he'd always been and his reaction to Edward had rammed that home. The kiss they'd shared just before Edward's appearance had shown her just how much she still cared for him. She knew a relationship between the two of them could never be and, besides, right now Edward was her first priority. 'Natural chemistry or not,' she said with finality. So why did she feel so...melancholy? 'This is no way to focus for your first day on the job. You're a professional.' With that, she set about showering and dressing, ready for the big day ahead.

'I found 'er, Mummy,' Edward called as she walked into the kitchen. 'I found Gr'ma,' he said and launched himself at his mother's legs. He grabbed hold of one, making it impossible for Julia to walk. She reached down to tickle him and he collapsed on the floor in a bundle of giggles.

'Morning, Mum.' Julia crossed to where her mother stood in the kitchen, putting the coffee on, and kissed her cheek.

'Ready for work?' Cassandra asked around a yawn. She was the same height as her daughter, five feet six inches, had short brown curls and green eyes. Julia's brown eyes had been inherited from her father just the way Edward's blue eyes were inherited from his father.

'As ready as I'll ever be.'

'To work with Zac, you mean.' Cassandra shook her head, a small smile playing around her lips.

'That's right. As of this morning, we're officially colleagues.'

Cassandra laughed. 'Do you honestly believe you'll be able to keep your relationship strictly professional?'

'He doesn't want children, Mum, and I have a child. I think that *might* put a dampener on anything that might flare up.'

'Wait and see, dear. You never know.'

'You've been watching too many romantic movies, Mum. No, Zac and I will just have to be...old friends. Nothing more.'

'With a frightening natural chemistry that still seems to exist,' her mother added.

'Just because we shared a couple of kisses—'

'Julia.' Cassandra tried interrupting.

'Doesn't mean—'

'Julia—I'm teasing you. Go and get Edward dressed while I finish making breakfast.'

'That anything is going to happen,' Julia finished. 'Besides, those kisses were *before* he knew about Edward.' She picked her son and his cars up off the floor. 'Come on, monkey. Time to get dressed.'

'No,' Edward protested, and wriggled a bit. Julia knew it was just for effect and that, whether he liked it or not, he was getting changed.

'What would you like to wear today? Green shorts or red shorts?'

'Um, gween.'

'And how about your aeroplane T-shirt?'

'Yes.'

Edward continued to play cars as Julia changed his

clothes. She didn't mind that her son's attention was occupied as her thoughts were still focused on Zac. If she closed her eyes, she could almost feel the touch of his lips on hers. The scent of his cologne, the way his arms had held her firmly against his chest. Zac made her feel…everything. Happy, cherished, beautiful, intelligent—everything. Now, though, she had to brush it all aside and be professional. It was the only way they were going to get through the next twelve months.

'Hold still, darling,' she said as her son wriggled.

Edward put his arms through the T-shirt holes and pronounced himself dressed. He ran off to show 'Gr'ma'.

'I dressed, I dressed, Gr'ma,' she heard him call, and her smile increased.

How could Zac *not* want children? They were so gorgeous, so lively, so full of unconditional love.

'Breakfast is ready,' her mother called as Julia washed her hands.

'Coming.' They ate breakfast as a family, both she and her mother delighting in Edward's antics. He was the apple of her eye and he had so much energy that she wished she could harness it and use it for herself!

She showered and dressed in khaki shorts and a white shirt before slipping her feet into a comfortable pair of flat shoes. Next, she brushed her curls and pulled them back into a plain ponytail.

'Make-up,' she said out loud, and looked at her reflection. Usually she wore only mascara as she generally didn't have time for beauty routines and hated the look of lipstick that was half worn off. Should she put full make-up on today?

'No,' she told herself, and quickly applied the mascara. 'Besides, Zac has seen you looking your worst a million times over so there's no need to impress him now!' She was also sure that he probably wouldn't care. When he looked at her, all he'd see was a single mother!

She brushed her teeth before packing her bag. When she was ready she went in search of Edward, who was busy driving a toy car over the packing boxes that littered the floor of their house.

She picked up another car and brought it over from the other side of the box.

'Hello,' she said, putting on a funny voice.

'Hello, car,' he replied, not looking at her but at the car she held. 'Where going?'

'Off to work.'

'Oh, good. I go work, too. Brrmmm,' he muttered, and drove his car off in the opposite direction, waiting for her to follow him. She did so, crawling around on her hands and knees.

They played like this for ten minutes until her mother said, 'It's a quarter to eight, Julia. Were you going to walk today?'

'Yes. Time for Mummy to go, darling,' she told her son, and pulled him into her arms.

'Mummy go work now?'

'Yes, darling. You have a good day with Grandma.'

'Yes.' He went back to his cars.

'Does Mummy get a kiss goodbye?'

'Yes,' he said again, and returned to her side. He placed his hands on either side of her face before pressing a sloppy kiss onto her lips.

'Ooh, I love you, honey-man.'

'Love you, too, Mummy,' he said matter-of-factly, and was glad when she released him so he could return to his cars.

She stood and looked at her mother. 'Have a good day. Are you going to the swimming pool?'

'We'll see how things go.'

'I'll give you a call later to let you know when to expect me home.'

'All right.' Cassandra hugged her daughter. 'Have a good day and don't worry about Zac. Everything will be fine.'

Julia forced a smile. 'I know.' Butterflies started to churn in her stomach as she blew kisses to her son, picked up her bag and walked out the door. It was a beautiful January morning that was simply perfect for a short walk to work. It wasn't too hot and the humidity hadn't yet reached its peak, which made Julia determined to enjoy it.

She looked at the beautiful gardens with their flowers in bloom, enjoying the sounds of birds chirping in the trees that lined the street. A car horn sounded behind her, breaking the moment, and she turned with a frown on her face to see who the culprit was.

'Zac!' The word lodged in her throat as she glared at him in surprise. She stopped walking as he pulled the Jag up to the kerb alongside her. The top on the car was down so she bore the full brunt of just how handsome he was. The butterflies in her stomach took flight at the sight of him. He was dressed in navy trousers, a blue and white striped shirt, with the sleeves rolled up, and a colourful tie. He looked...wonderful.

'Julia,' he said with a nod, not a smile in sight. 'Would you like a lift?'

'Ah...no, thanks. I'm enjoying the walk.' Good girl, she praised herself. She'd decided not to do anything out of the ordinary towards him and compromising her walk would have been doing just that.

'Sure.' His gaze travelled over her shorts and top, lingering on her legs. He'd *loved* her legs back when they'd been dating and it seemed he felt the same about *that* at least. 'Well, in that case,' he said as he brought his gaze back to meet hers, 'I won't intrude any longer.' He flashed her a smile before revving the engine and driving off up the street.

Julia was stunned at the speed of his exit. Obviously he didn't find her too distracting!

When she arrived at the hospital, Zac was standing at the front entrance, waiting for her, a forced smile on his handsome face, his blue gaze showing concern.

He looked so cute that Julia had to laugh. His smile turned curious but at least it was natural.

'What?' he asked as she came to stand beside him.

'You haven't changed.'

'What's that supposed to mean?' he asked in a low whisper, a slight defensive edge to his tone.

'It simply means, my dear Zachary, that there are some things about you that will always be the same.'

'Like what?' he asked as he gestured for them to start walking. 'We'll be late for ward round,' he explained, and she nodded. 'So, like what?' he asked again when she didn't answer.

'Fishing?' she teased. She felt happy and giddy, like a schoolgirl, teasing Zac again.

'No. Trying to get a straight answer,' he replied with a chuckle, and she was glad she'd been able to lift his dark mood. 'In that way *you* haven't changed. Always beating about the bush.'

'Only with you,' she confirmed. 'It's one of my greatest assets.'

'One of them,' he murmured softly as they went through the doors to the orthopaedic ward.

'Like my legs?' she asked pointedly, her tone matching his.

Zac stopped walking and placed a hand on her arm to

stop her as well. He looked down into her eyes and swallowed, his Adam's apple working up and down. Julia swallowed, too.

Their gazes held and for a moment she felt as though they were the only two people on earth. Her mother had been absolutely correct when she'd described it as a frightening natural chemistry. It also appeared that they were both struggling to control it!

'Zac?' a strange female voice called. The spell was broken and both looked away. 'You were almost late, Zac,' the other woman chastised lightly. She had short blonde hair and blue eyes—eyes that were boring into Julia with curiosity. 'Aren't you going to introduce us?' she queried, and held out her hand to Julia.

'Of course,' he said, and cleared his throat. 'Tess Marshall, this is Julia Bolton. Julia's our new orthopaedic surgeon.'

'I see.' Tess raised her eyebrows, her smile plastered firmly in place. 'Welcome, Julia. I'm the ward sister. We're all rather informal about the hospital, aren't we, Zac?' She didn't look at him as she spoke, obviously preferring to keep Julia firmly in her sights.

'That's right, and as it's just after eight, we'd better start the ward round.' He turned and walked down the corridor, leaving both women to follow.

Julia left her bag at the nurses' station when the round began. Gold Coast General was quite a bit smaller than her previous hospital, with this ward being the only orthopaedic ward for both children and adults alike. At her hospital in Perth, there had been four orthopaedic wards and that had just been for the adults. Paediatric orthopaedics was done at a different hospital.

She smiled as they came to a young boy of about seven who was in for observation after falling out of a tree and fracturing his right radius, ulna and humerus. The radiographs of his skull had shown a hairline fracture to the frontal lobe, but from all reports he was doing just fine.

He seemed a bit daunted by having so many people crowding around his bed—interns, medical students, nurses, registrars, as well as Zac and herself.

'I think you can go home later today, Timmy.' Zac smiled genuinely at the child.

Timmy was playing with some toy cars, similar to the ones Edward played with. Julia had been astounded by her son and his love for cars. Not once had she encouraged him or put one in his hands, but he loved them. She only supposed it was genetic!

'Wow, an F-40 Ferrari,' she said excitedly. 'That's a really cool car,' Julia added, and Timmy smiled. She walked up beside his bed and he held it out for her inspection. 'May I have a look, please?'

'My dad bought it for me,' he said. 'And this one, too. It's a Mustang convertible.'

'Dr Zac here drives a convertible,' she told him. 'A Jaguar XK8,' she added.

'Wow!' Timmy's eyes grew wide as he looked at Zac. 'That's wicked!'

'Sure is,' Zac agreed. 'You keep getting better, Timmy,' he said, making a quick note on the boy's chart. 'I'll see you in my clinic in two weeks' time, OK?'

'Yep,' Timmy replied, and waved secretly to Julia as they all moved off to see the next patient.

When the round was done, Julia collected her bag from the nurses' station and was about to walk out when she looked up to find Tess in front of her.

'Oh, sorry.' She smiled at the nurse. 'I didn't see you there.'

'How do you know what type of car Zac drives?' Tess asked, her tone accusing.

'Well, I was walking to work this morning and he stopped and offered me a lift.'

'But,' Tess countered with a smug smile, 'I saw him drive into the hospital grounds and he was alone.'

'Yes, he was. I told him I was enjoying my morning walk and he...' she shrugged '...drove off.'

'Without you?'

'Yes. Some people have no manners.'

'Julia,' Zac called, stopping Tess from saying anything more on the subject, 'let's go check on Mr Ishimaru or we'll be late for clinic. I don't want you getting lost on your first day.' He smiled at Tess, but no differently than he did to the other members of the nursing staff.

'She has a crush on you,' Julia said as they walked away. She could feel Tess glaring after them.

He groaned. 'I know.'

'What are you going to do?'

'Easy. I'll put my arm around your shoulders, ease you back over my arm and plant a great big smoochy kiss on your lips. That should do the trick.'

Julia was horrified and stopped walking. 'You will not.' Then she caught the teasing glint in his eye. She smiled and shook her head as they continued out of the ward. 'As I said, Zac, some things never change!'

Next they went to the critical care unit to check on Aki Ishimaru. 'He was holding his own quite well yesterday,' Zac said as they walked quietly into the ward. 'I had to reinsert a drain yesterday morning but since then he's had no complications.' They read the nursing notes before one of the nurses accompanied them over to the patient.

Aki lay there, still and expressionless. He was healing well from his surgery and Zac was satisfied. His asthma was under control and the nursing staff were happy with his progress.

'See if it's possible to have the Japanese translator here tomorrow morning for ward round,' he asked. 'If there's any problem, let me know.'

After writing up Aki's notes, Zac and Julia headed for clinic.

It didn't take long for Julia to find her way about the clinic so long as she followed her golden rule—when in doubt, ask a member of the nursing staff. They always knew what was going on or where things were kept.

Zac had quickly introduced her to the staff as they'd walked through the crowded waiting room. She read up the previous entries in each patient's notes before calling them into her room. The process, naturally, took a bit longer but as there were Zac, one orthopaedic registrar and herself doing the clinic, they managed to finish on time.

'Ready for lunch?'

Zac's deep voice washed over her and she looked up to see him lounging in the doorway. Her gaze slowly travelled the length of him, starting with his shoes and ending with his face. His smile was sexy and his eyes were filled with repressed desire. She felt a warmth spread through her and her heart rate increase its rhythm.

'Starving,' she said, and couldn't believe how husky her voice had sounded. The man was only asking her about lunch—or was he? She forced herself to concentrate on writing up the notes of her last patient while trying to control her rising libido.

Zac waited patiently for her to finish and when she'd placed the case notes in the appropriate tray for filing, she stood and looked at him. The smile had gone from his face and the look in his eyes had only intensified.

'So how was it?' His voice was as smooth as silk.

Julia's gaze held his. Why did everything he say appear to be filled with innuendo?

She knew he was talking about the clinic, at least on a conscious level, but she decided to tease him a little instead. She took her brush out of her bag and pulled her hair free from its band, brushing her curls, knowing how much Zac used to love her hair loose.

Watching his reaction closely, she was pleased to see him tug at the knot of his tie and clear his throat. It appeared Dr Carmichael *still* liked her hair loose. Of course, back then it had been a lot longer, but now she actually preferred it at its current easier-to-manage shoulder length.

Closing her eyes, Julia scooped the hair back into her usual ponytail and wound the band around. When she had finished, she glanced at him before replacing her brush and picking up her bag.

She walked slowly towards him, knowing he wouldn't move from the doorway he still blocked.

'It was...good,' she whispered, and stood before him. 'How about you? Was it good for you, too?'

A slow smile spread over Zac's face and he cleared his throat. 'Are you flirting with me, Dr Bolton?' His tone was quiet.

'And what if I am?' she asked.

Zac took a deep breath and stood. 'I think it's time I showed you your office.' He turned on his heel and they walked out of clinic together. They headed down the corridor towards the administrative offices of the surgical departments.

'You're next to me,' he said as they walked along.

'Yes, I am. How astute of you, Zac!'

His smile widened. 'I've missed your sense of humour, Jules. I meant, in offices.'

'Oh.' She laughed. They came to a door and Zac swiped

his hospital identification badge through it. He waited for the click, indicating that the door had been released, before pushing it open. 'Ah, I see Jeffrey's been here,' she said, pointing to the security device.

'Yes. How did you know?' he asked as he held the door for her before they walked past several offices.

'At Perth General, where we both worked, there was a huge break-in and hundreds of patient files were stolen. I'm sure it made the news. Anyway, as a result, Jeffrey, who was acting hospital director, made the decision to have any area where patient files were stored fitted with a security device similar to that one.'

'I thought it might have been something like that,' he said as he unlocked a door and pushed it open. 'This is it.'

Julia walked into the room and put her bag down on the desk. She opened the blinds, letting daylight flood into the room. There was already a pile of waiting files on her desk and she groaned when she saw them.

'Your inheritance,' Zac announced with a smile as he saw her grimace. He nudged the door closed with his foot and came to stand behind her. He ran his hands tenderly up her arms, his thumbs massaging her shoulders. Julia held her breath, her eyelids fluttering closed as his lips pressed lightly to her neck, the slight graze from his stubbled jaw continuing to fuel the fire that was burning within her. She groaned as the small butterfly kisses caused goose-bumps to spread throughout her body.

'You smell so incredible, Julia. You're driving me wild.'

Julia clung to his words with hope. Did this mean that Zac *wanted* to date her? Even though she was a single mother?

'No,' he groaned, and let her go. For an instant she

thought she'd asked the question out loud. 'No,' he repeated.

Julia's elation vanished and she turned to look at him. His hands were held up as he slowly backed towards the door—putting distance between them.

Julia squared her shoulders and cleared her throat. 'So what's it to be, Zac? Friends or just professional colleagues?'

His gaze met hers and she fought against the fire he could ignite within her at a mere look. 'Friends, Julia. We've always been good...friends.'

Julia could hear her heart beat pounding furiously in her ears. 'Sure,' she heard herself say. 'Strictly platonic. No problem.' She forced a smile and nodded again, cursing the tears that were stinging in her eyes.

'Oh, Jules,' he ground out as he covered the distance between them. His mouth met hers with a mutual need— a hunger so intense it momentarily robbed her of breath.

Julia thrust her fingers into his hair, holding his head firmly in place. She'd dreamed of this ever since their last kiss early Sunday morning. She felt so right in his arms; their bodies melded together with perfect symmetry.

His lips were hot and possessive over hers, his hands sliding firmly up and down her back while he held her close. This wasn't a kiss of friendship, her sluggish brain realised. The attraction that flared between them was so natural, so...right. Were they wrong to try and deny it?

He groaned and pulled away but Julia urged his head back down and kissed him again. Zac had the most masterful mouth she'd ever kissed. As their hunger gave way to passion, he teased and nipped at her lips, causing a flood of tingles to burst throughout her body.

His hands moved slowly from her back around to her front. The sides of his thumbs lightly grazed her breasts, causing Julia to gasp with wonderment. His hands continued up her arms to disengage her fingers from his hair. All the while, their lips were still seeking and evoking a mutual response.

He held her hands in his and pressed them to his chest. Julia was slightly conscious of feeling the rapid rate of his heartbeat. Slowly, reluctantly, Zac edged his mouth away from hers to gaze down into her eyes which she knew were as clouded with desire as his own.

Both were breathing heavily, his grip on her hands firm and controlled. He raised her fingers to his lips and kissed each one tenderly. Julia's eyes fluttered closed as a new round of sensations spread through her. The last finger he held longer than the others, his tongue circling it before he sucked it between his lips.

Gathering her close, he kissed her forehead and rested her head against his chest. They stood there for a few minutes as their breathing gradually settled back to a normal rhythm. When Julia felt her legs would support her she pushed against his chest and he reluctantly let her go.

'That felt like...' She stopped and took a breath. 'Like a goodbye kiss.'

'It was.' With that, he dropped his arms and crossed to the door. Without looking back, he opened the door, walked through and closed it behind him, leaving her feeling desolate and destroyed.

# CHAPTER FOUR

AN HOUR later, Julia had read several of the case-notes in front of her, trying desperately to focus her mind on work, rather than Zac.

The man was just as stubborn as he'd always been. 'Friends,' she mumbled, and leaned back in her chair. The attraction between them had always been strong—so strong, in fact, that Julia had fled to the other side of the country when she and Zac had finally parted.

Julia closed her eyes, remembering when she'd flown to Sydney to talk to him. They hadn't seen each other for a whole week, and when she'd arrived he'd been in Theatre. Her nervousness had grown, knowing that there was a lot riding on what they had to discuss. By the time Zac had finished in Theatre, Julia had been a mass of nerves. Yet the instant they'd seen each other, Zac had quickly covered the distance between them and in one swift movement had gathered her into his arms and pressed his mouth hungrily to her own.

'Zac,' she'd sighed, winding her arms lovingly about his neck. She had been amazed that after all the time they'd spent together, the attraction had still been as new and exciting as in the beginning.

'You're a sight for sore eyes,' he'd whispered when they'd finally broken apart. 'I'm all done here. So where would you like to go tonight?'

'Actually, Zac...we really need to sort things out.'

'*Now*, Jules? I've just finished a long stint in Theatre

and don't know if I have the energy to go another round with you.'

'Can we discuss this somewhere other than the corridor outside Theatres?'

They went to the little cubicle that was classified as his office. 'Ding, ding,' he said, hitting an imaginary boxing bell. 'Let round fifty-two begin.'

'You're exaggerating, again,' she chided, unable to hide her smile. 'I need to make a decision about where I'm going to be working in the future.'

'So? Make the decision. You're a big girl.'

That made her angry. 'Come off it, Zac. Do you really want me to accept the job in Perth? On the other side of the country?'

'You have to do what's right for *you*, Jules.'

'So you don't feel that you figure in the equation at all?'

He took her hand in his. 'Julia, you have a lot to give and I don't want to stand in the way of you doing what you need to do. You'd end up resenting me one day and I never want that to happen.'

'Oh don't give me that, Zac.' She pulled away from him. 'That's just a cop-out. You just don't want to make a commitment—a permanent commitment,' she amended when he opened his mouth to protest. 'You've known from the start that I've always wanted to get married, to have a family. I'm not talking about right *now* but some time in the future.'

He shrugged. 'I'm just not the family type of guy, Jules. Sure, I like kids but when they're someone else's. Marriage just isn't for me.'

'You're scared, Zac.'

'I am not.'

'You are. Just because your parents' marriage broke up, you think the same thing is going to happen to you.'

'That's not true—'

'That's part of the problem,' she interrupted. 'You have to at least acknowledge that much.'

'What if it is,' he finally said. 'It still doesn't change the fact that I'm more interested in my career, in travelling, in having new medical experiences. I can't do that if I have a family hanging around my neck.'

His words acted like a verbal slap and Julia recoiled. 'So you think that if we get married, I'd drag you down.'

'That's not what I said, Julia.' He reached out to take her hand again but she moved away. 'Julia.'

'No, Zac. I love you.' Tears had gathered in her eyes and her tone held a hint of desperation.

'I love you, too. That's why I don't want to stand in your way.'

'Oh...so you're going to go on the if-you-love-someone-set-them-free, tack?' She shook her head, tears spilling onto her cheeks. 'We've always brought out the best in each other,' she whispered as she backed towards the door. 'We are so *right*, so *perfect* for each other, but you obviously can't see that.'

Julia opened the door, her blurry gaze fixed on the man she loved with all her heart. 'Goodbye, Zac.' Her voice cracked as she said his name, and before she could change her mind, Julia turned and ran out of the hospital, knowing he wouldn't pursue her but hoping he would just the same.

Julia opened her eyes and breathed in deeply. Even now, the hurt he'd caused was still so alive in her memory. Still, she'd managed to get on with her life then and she could do the same now.

But this was only her first day at work! They still had the rest of the year to get through. That kiss they'd just shared had been incredible. It had been everything and more than she remembered.

But she had changed a lot since leaving him ten years ago, just as she knew he'd changed also. Some things, though, remained the same, like the easy camaraderie they'd always shared. Yes, they'd always been good friends so perhaps they could share that again.

Julia sighed and collected some money from her bag. 'First things first—lunch.' She crossed to her door and opened it, jumping with fright when she was faced with solid male on the other side.

'Sorry. Didn't mean to startle you,' Zac said. 'I was about to knock.'

They stood looking at each other for a few moments and Julia desperately tried to think of something to say. The money jingled in her hand and she looked down. 'Ah, I was just about to get something to eat.'

He nodded. 'Right. Well, I need you—'

Julia dropped her money on the floor and they both bent to pick it up. Their hands touched and she quickly jerked hers away as though he'd burnt her. He gave her a cautious look before straightening, letting her pick up the coins. She forced her gaze not to look at his gorgeous body as she stood, forced herself not to be affected by him, forced herself to lie. She couldn't do it.

She cleared her throat. 'You were saying, Zac? You need me?'

'To come to Theatre. With me. This afternoon.' He cleared his throat and ran his finger around the collar of his shirt.

'I thought I had the afternoon to complete the hospital red tape. You know, identification badge, pager, and so on. I'm not...all wired up.'

'It'll have to wait. I need you. I need to do a pelvic fracture operation and it's scheduled for today.'

'I see. What's the history? MVA?'

'Hit-and-run victim. Eight days ago, thirty-nine-year-old female, Bianca Hayden, was hit as she hurried across the road. She sustained a fracture to her right humerus, cracked the right fourth, fifth and sixth ribs, as well as the left fifth and sixth.' He was in 'doctor' mode and she listened intently to what he was saying.

'I've set a Grosse and Kempf nail down her right femur and debrided and strapped the third and forth phalanges on her right foot. Urology fixed her ruptured bladder and urethra.'

'Sounds like she's had a great time,' Julia said ironically, shaking her head. 'The poor woman.'

'Generally, I like to give the pelvis a chance to settle to see whether surgical intervention is necessary, which in this case it is. I knew I'd have extra help today so that's why I put her on the list.'

'OK. Do you want to go over the operation, then?'

'Sure, but get some lunch first and meet me in my office.'

'Great.' Zac smiled at her, a genuine smile that said he was feeling a little more comfortable. 'Can I get you anything, Zac?'

'No. I'm fine.' Zac didn't move. He just stood there, looking at her. His pager beeped, startling both of them. 'I'll just go answer this.'

'OK. Oh, Zac—how do I get to the cafeteria?'

His smile increased and he gave her directions.

'Thanks.' Julia headed for the door.

'Jules,' Zac called, and she turned in time to see him toss his hospital identification badge at her. She caught it and smiled. 'You'll be needing that to get back in,' he said.

'Thanks,' she said again and walked out of the department. She found the cafeteria without complication and bought her lunch. When she returned to his office, she'd already finished half of her sandwich. She walked through the open door, sat down opposite him and placed his badge on the desk.

'Feeling better?'

She nodded and swallowed her mouthful. 'Food always makes me feel better.'

'I remember,' he said softly. 'I also remember you nearly passing out on me one night when we were all studying, due to lack of food.'

Julia smiled with remembrance. 'You came down on me like a ton of bricks for not looking after myself, and I'm pleased to report that I've never been that bad since,' she told him. 'Your lecture worked.'

He seemed surprised. 'Good.' He broke eye contact and stood, crossing the room to switch on the X-ray viewing box on his wall before hooking some radiographs up.

'Three-dimensional scanning,' she said, impressed. 'That'll certainly help.'

'It does. CT scanning is good but this way I get an entire look at what's *really* happening with the fractures and can pinpoint exactly where they are. Then I use this.' He took some Plasticine out of his top drawer. 'I roll this out so it's quite thin and then, using a plastic pelvis...' He pointed to a shelf behind him and Julia turned to look. There were all sorts of bones and she picked up a replica of the female pelvis and handed it to him. 'I place the Plasticine where the fracture is and then I have a complete image that I can pick up and turn over in my hands to know exactly how to fix the fracture.'

'Ingenious,' she said, knowing he was waiting for her praise.

'Thank you. Take a look at this first scan.'

'Fracture of the right hemipelvis involving the sacroiliac

joint, acetabular and pubic rami and symphysis bilaterally. Tough one.'

'That's why I need two surgeons,' he pointed out. 'Have you done any pelvic fracture operations before?' he asked.

'A few. I studied over in France during my final year of orthopaedic training.'

'With Professor LaCourte?'

'Yes.' Julia finished her sandwich before neatly lobbing the paper into the bin behind him.

'Now *I'm* impressed.'

'What? With my basketball skills?'

He chuckled. 'No. Working with LaCourte. He's one of the world's leading pelvic fracture surgeons.'

'Thank you,' she replied, suddenly feeling extra special because of his praise.

Zac looked at her and shook his head.

'What?'

'There's so much about you that I don't know.'

'Ditto!' There was silence again before Zac crossed back to his desk and began rolling out Plasticine. 'So what approaches were you planning on using?'

'Ilioinguinal then Kocher-Langenbeck.'

Julia nodded. 'Great.'

'So you approve?'

She gave him a quizzical look. 'Why wouldn't I?'

'Well, you're the one who's studied with the experts in France.'

She smiled. 'Feeling a bit intimidated?'

'No.'

'You're lying, Zac. This is me you're talking to. When you get annoyed, you clench your jaw and grind your teeth. When you're frustrated, you run your hand through your hair or put your hands in your pockets. When you're uncomfortable or, dare I say it, intimidated, you rub your chin with your finger and thumb.'

As she said the words, Zac absent-mindedly lifted his hand and did exactly what she said he'd do. He narrowed his gaze and instantly dropped his hand.

'That's not fair,' he mumbled.

'Come on, Zachary.' Julia tried not to laugh. 'You know things about me. How I pass out if I don't get a regular intake of food—that sort of thing.' She watched as he raked his hand through his hair, smiling to herself. 'It's only natural.'

When he looked at her again, he shook his head. 'Stop it. Stop getting inside my head.'

'I'm not doing it on purpose,' she offered as she stood and crossed to his side. 'Hold still,' she instructed. 'You have Plasticine in your hair.'

Zac couldn't have moved, even if he'd wanted to. Her close proximity had taken him by surprise, and as she moved in closer, he found his gaze level with her breasts. He groaned inwardly and closed his eyes, feeling her fingers brushing against his scalp. Desire flooded him instantly and he called on every ounce of will-power he possessed to stop himself from dragging her down onto his lap and kissing her senseless.

'There you go,' she said softly, and drew back. She showed him the offending piece of Plasticine before throwing it into the bin.

'Thanks.' His voice was deep and husky. He cleared his throat and tossed her a ball of Plasticine. 'Here. Roll this.'

Julia did as he asked and together they pieced the fracture together on the plastic bone, discussing the operation as they worked. When they were done, they locked their respective offices and headed towards Elective Theatres.

Zac pointed the way to the female changing rooms but had no idea what the security code was to enter.

'That's new. Time was you'd have made it your business to find out the number for the female changing rooms,' she teased.

He returned her smile. 'Times have changed.'

She merely shrugged. 'I'll find someone and ask them what the code is.' She smiled and headed off back down the corridor. Julia introduced herself to a theatre nurse and asked for the code. After being assigned a locker and collecting theatre scrubs, she quickly changed and went in search of a phone.

'Hi, Mum.'

'How's it going, dear?'

'Fine and dandy,' Julia replied. 'I'm about to go into Theatre for the afternoon so I anticipate being home around eight or nine o'clock. Hopefully it won't take that long.'

'Sounds like a serious accident,' Cassandra said.

'Pelvic fracture reconstruction.'

'I see. Well, let me get Edward so you can talk to him.'

While she waited for her son to come to the phone she turned to see Zac coming up the corridor towards her.

'Problem?' he asked, and she shook her head.

'Hi, Mummy,' Edward's voice said down the line.

'Hello, darling,' she said softly. 'Are you having a good day?' Julia watched as Zac's expression turned bland.

'I'll leave you to it,' he mumbled, and continued on his way.

'Yes.'

Julia watched Zac go, determined not to apologise for wanting to speak to her son. It wasn't interfering with her work so he couldn't be angry with her for that. Still, he'd clenched his jaw and ground his teeth as he'd walked off.

She returned her attention to Edward. 'What did you and Grandma do?'

'Um.' He thought. 'Lunch.'

'You had lunch, did you?'

'Yes.'

'Did you have jam on your sandwich?'

'Yes,' he replied again. Julia closed her eyes and smiled.

'Mummy's going to be late home tonight so you go to bed when Grandma says, OK?'

'Oh-tay.'

'I love you, honey-man.'

'Love you, Mummy,' he said, and blew a noisy kiss down the phone. Julia jerked the receiver away from her ear momentarily so his 'kiss' didn't damage her eardrum.

'He's full of beans today,' Cassandra said as she came back on the line. 'I thought I'd take him down the road to that park we saw the other day and take him to the pool tomorrow.'

'Good idea. As I said, I'll try not to be too late.'

'Will you be all right, getting home in the dark?'

Julia thought for a moment. 'I'll take a taxi. It's not that far.'

'Perhaps Zac can drive you home,' her mother suggested.

'Ha! Good one, Mum. Some days you're so funny. You forget that I'm the single mother to be avoided at all costs.'

'What's happened?' Cassandra asked.

'He's given me the let's-be-friends speech.'

'Already? That was fast. Never mind.'

'Oh, I'm not.'

'Yes, dear,' her mother said indulgently.

Julia ignored it. 'I'd better go and find out where I'm supposed to be. Bye, Mum.' She rang off and headed in the direction Zac had gone.

'There you are,' he said as she rounded the corner. His gaze met hers briefly but she didn't need to look deeply into his eyes to know that he was annoyed. His fingers were clenched, due to lack of pockets in theatre scrubs, and there wasn't even a hint of a smile on his face. 'We're in Theatre Two,' he told her as he stalked off, leaving her to follow.

At the scrub sink, there was a theatre nurse as well as Rodney, one of the orthopaedic registrars. The scrub nurse helped them gown up.

'For those of you who haven't met, this is Dr Julia Bolton, our new orthopaedic surgeon,' Zac said in his best professional tone.

The theatre and scrub nurses murmured their greetings and Rodney just smiled at her.

'Let's get started.' Zac and the rest of the staff entered Theatre where Bianca Hayden, their patient, was anaesthetised and waiting. 'You know Lucille from the other day,' he said, motioning with his head to the anaesthetist.

'Hi, Julia. Nice to see you again.'

'Likewise.'

'Jeffrey told me that you used to work with him at Perth General Hospital,' Lucille said.

'That's right. He was only acting hospital director then.'

'So that's how you heard we desperately needed another orthopod,' Theatre Sister said, and nodded her head.

'Exactly. Four weeks ago, I was deliberating whether to renew my contract and then I received a phone call from Jeffrey. He told me about the job, and as he knew my credentials he recommended me. Three weeks later—here I am!'

'He's the best hospital director we've had here,' Theatre Sister continued as the patient was draped and swabbed, ready for Zac's initial incision.

'How long had you been at Perth General?' Lucille asked.

'Far too long,' Julia murmured.

'Needed a change?'

'It was either move across the country or take on the position as head of the orthopaedic department,' she told them, knowing Zac was finding all of this very interesting.

'You didn't want to be head of department?' he asked, trying to make his voice sound casual. He was surprised that as she'd only been a qualified surgeon for three years, she would be offered such a position. Then again, he'd only been qualified for four years and here he was, head of an orthopaedic department. However, this hospital was quite a bit smaller than the one she'd worked at in Perth.

'No,' she replied, not looking at him. 'Why bother with the extra aggravation and stress? I can do without those headaches, thank you very much.'

'Interesting,' he said softly, but Julia heard.

Surely he wasn't threatened by her professionally? It was true that she'd only been qualified for three years but she'd done a lot during that time. She'd been nine weeks pregnant when she'd caught Ian in bed with yet another floozy and had thrown him out. The next day, she'd filed for a separation and had arranged with the hospital to change her working schedule.

She'd obtained a research grant and had done a lot of work from home during Edward's first year of life, only going into the hospital for clinics, meetings and her scheduled operating sessions. Jeffrey and Mona had been a great support, as well as her mother, so it had been no wonder she'd won the prize for best research paper at last year's American orthopaedic conference.

It might have only been three years but as she'd been pregnant and raising a child, Julia was prodigiously proud of her accomplishments. And if Zac was threatened by them, that was *his* problem.

'Ready to incise,' he said, bringing her focus back to the operation at hand. His first incision was for the anterior ilioinguinal approach, and once the fractures had been exposed they cleared the edges.

They worked together quite efficiently, with Julia able to anticipate his next move and have everything ready. When the fractures had been reduced and fixed with two reconstructive plates, they readied themselves for the Kocher-Langenbeck approach.

Again they exposed the fractures and cleared the edges before applying one more reconstructive plate posteriorly as well as an interfragmentary screw near the acetabular margin.

'Ready for a check X-ray,' Zac said some five hours later. While he waited for the radiographer to perform her task, he walked over to take another look at the three-dimensional scans up on the viewing box. Julia came up beside him.

'I think the X-ray will show everything to be fine,' she told him, and he turned to look at her.

'A job well done,' he agreed. The time in surgery had helped the annoyance—on both sides—to disappear.

Once the radiograph was processed, they both peered at the film. 'Excellent,' Zac announced. 'Let's get ready to close.'

They closed in layers of number one Vicryl, then double zero Vicryl before stapling the wound closed. It had been almost one-thirty in the afternoon when they'd started the operation and, as Julia had predicted to her mother, it was almost eight o'clock as she changed out of her theatre garb back into her clothes.

She returned to her office, only to remember she needed

a hospital identification badge to swipe through the slot to enter the admin area. She'd have to wait for Zac but he might not come back this way before heading home. So Julia headed back towards Theatres in search of him. She'd left him writing up the operation notes but knew he still needed to change.

As she rounded a corner in the corridor towards the theatre block, she saw a man down the other end, coming towards her. Her heart pounded with delight and she knew that even if the corridor had been crowded, she still would have been able to pick Zac's military precision walk anywhere. She stopped and waited for him to catch up, a smile on his face.

'Going my way?' he asked as she fell into step beside him. He didn't seem at all surprised to see her, and she realised that he'd known she'd be waiting.

'I can't get into the department,' she replied.

'I know,' he said, and waved his hospital badge under her nose. 'We'll rectify it first thing in the morning.' Zac stopped at the door and swiped his card through. 'You'd best keep the key to your office as well,' he said after he'd unlocked her door. He took the key off the ring while he waited for her to collect her bag.

'Here.' He pressed it into her palm, his fingers enveloping her hand for a fraction of a second longer than necessary. 'Can I offer you a lift?'

Julia smiled, remembering her mother's words. 'Thanks, Zac. I'd appreciate it.'

He made no other attempt to touch her as they walked through the quietened hospital out to the doctors' car park. The roof of his Jag was up to protect the inside of the car from the warm January sun. Now that the sun had set, she wondered whether he'd put it down again. Like the gentleman he'd always been, Zac unlocked and held the door for her.

'Thank you,' she said as she sat and did up her seat belt. He walked around the rear of the car and seated himself beside her.

'This is getting to be a habit, Dr Bolton,' he said.

'What? Driving me home?' When he nodded, she continued, 'I doubt I'd call twice a habit, Zachary.'

He merely smiled at her and started the car. 'Don't you have a car yet?' he asked as they drove out of the hospital grounds.

'Yes.'

'I thought you might have sold your car in Perth and not managed to buy one here, and that's why you walked to work this morning.'

'No. I have a car.'

'Does it work?'

She laughed. 'Yes, Zac, it works. I just felt like walking this morning and I might even feel like walking tomorrow morning.'

'From what I can recall,' he said, his brow furrowing a bit, 'you never used to be a morning person, yet here you're up and ready for work with enough time to spare to enjoy a leisurely walk. I remember you struggling to make a nine o'clock lecture!'

She smiled and nodded. 'There are a lot of things about me that have changed since you saw me last.'

'So I'm noticing.'

She knew he was referring to Edward by the tone of his voice, but once again she refused to apologise for having a child. He turned the car into her street and slowed as they neared her house. As he'd done the other evening, he stopped the car and climbed out to open her door.

'I'll bet there are a lot of differences in you,' Julia said as he walked her to the door. 'It's been twelve years since you moved from Brisbane to Sydney and two years after that was the last time I saw you, until the other night. That's ten years we've not physically seen each other, Zac, and during that time a *lot* of things have happened to change the idealistic people we were back then.'

'The chemistry is still alive, though,' he said softly, keeping his distance.

Julia nodded. 'Yeah, there's that but, honestly, Zac, is it going to be enough? I think you were right today when you said we should just be friends. There may be this physical attraction between us but during the past ten years we've met different people who have changed our views, our perceptions and ultimately, for better or worse, changed who we used to be.'

'Your ex-husband, for instance.'

'Exactly. Ian has changed me in so many ways, not because he was a nice man—he wasn't—but it's made me come out of my shell. To stand up for myself, not only at work but within my private life as well.'

'Did he abuse you?'

Julia thought for a moment before shaking her head. 'Not in the physical sense of the word, nor was it verbal abuse. He just...insulted my intelligence by thinking I'd put up with his affairs and keep quiet, but Ian isn't the point here. Surely you've had relationships that have changed who you used to be. They may have even changed some strong opinions you used to hold.'

His face was like a mask and for all she knew about him, Julia couldn't read his expression at all. He did nod, however, acknowledging her words.

'I know you've never wanted marriage or a family, Zac,' she said softly. 'And the fact that I have a son means we can never...' She trailed off. She looked down at her hands and then back to him. 'Thanks for the ride. See you tomorrow.'

Before she succumbed to the temptation to press her mouth to his, Julia quickly unlocked her front door and slipped inside.

Zac stared at the closed door for a full minute before slowly turning and walking back to his car. He drove home on autopilot and rode the lift up to his apartment. Julia represented everything he didn't want. A wife, a family. It was all too hard. Losing Cara had been so devastating that Zac had sworn to never again set himself up for that kind of misery.

Yet Julia made him think. The physical attraction between them made him think—and at the moment the last thing he wanted to do was think. Then there was the problem of her son. A son! Julia had a son!

As Zac checked the contents of his refrigerator, staring unseeingly at the food inside, he realised he shouldn't have been so surprised that she'd had a child. She'd always said she'd wanted to start a family one day. He shut the fridge and leaned against the bench.

It was the reason they'd broken up in the first place. Julia had wanted a more permanent commitment and he'd been unable to give it to her. She had been absolutely right to ask him straight out what his future plans were. The problem had been that they hadn't matched hers.

His ambition had been too great. He'd wanted to be the best he could be and damn the consequences. He'd realised that a wife with ambition had had no place in his life and as he hadn't been able to stand women who *didn't* have ambition, that had left him at an impasse. What a fool he'd been!

During the two years that he'd been in Sydney and Julia in Brisbane, they'd changed and grown apart a little. If she had taken the job on offer in Sydney, he had no doubt they would have settled their differences and stayed together—except that Julia had planned to one day start a family.

Zac looked at his answering machine and saw the flashing light. Knowing it couldn't be too urgent, otherwise the caller would have phoned his mobile, Zac pressed the button and waited for the tape to rewind.

'Zac, it's Jeffrey. Call me at home when you get in.'

Grabbing his cordless phone and sinking into the comfortable lounge, Zac kicked off his shoes as he pressed the speed dial for Jeffrey's home number.

'Jeffrey McArthur.'

'It's Zac.' He wearily took off his tie and undid the top few buttons of his shirt. Leaning back on the lounge, he stuffed a few pillows behind his head and put his feet up on the arm rest.

'Busy day?'

'Yep. What's up?'

'Nothing major. Just wanted to see how things went with Julia. You know, Cupid giving a follow-up call.'

'I've got to give you credit for taking me by surprise.'

'So, how are things going?'

'Good. We work well together but, then, I'm not surprised. Julia's a very smart woman.'

'Do you have any idea of what she's been through in the past few years?'

'Divorce? Pregnancy?'

'Ah. So you know about Edward?'

'Yep. Met him yesterday morning—only briefly. Cute kid.'

'Julia married my cousin, Ian. I warned her about him, almost ruined our friendship, but she was blinded by his lies. Then when she discovers him sleeping around once again, she kicks him out. *Then* she finds herself pregnant with a child Ian wants nothing to do with. He told her to get an abortion—can you believe that?' Jeffrey's tone was filled with disgust. 'He even had the audacity to try to deny paternity. She receives no support from him and he wants nothing to do with Edward.'

'Why are you telling me this?' Zac closed his eyes, trying to relax, but what Jeffrey was saying made him think even more.

'Because *she* won't. I have so much respect for that woman, Zac, that I want you to cut her a break. I know you've vowed never to marry again, not to let yourself get hurt, but just be there for her, mate. Coming back to Queensland was just what she needed and I want it to work out.' Jeffrey paused. 'Did you know she was offered head of department at Perth General?'

'Yes, actually, I did. She mentioned it in Theatre today and I thought it odd she should have been offered such a position in such a large teaching hospital.'

'It's because she's brilliant. When she realised she'd be raising her child by herself, she applied for and was successful in obtaining a research grant. She worked from home but still managed to keep up one clinic and operating session a week and wrote up her Ph.D. Last year, she won the prize for best overall paper at the American conference.'

Zac opened his eyes in astonishment. 'That was *her*? I read that paper. It was amazing.' He paused. 'I didn't take note of the primary author. What an oversight!'

'I'll say. Zac, her son is equally amazing. Edward has been raised in a loving and caring environment by his mother and grandmother and at not one stage along the way has he suffered from emotional neglect. Give him a chance, too. Get to know him, Zac. He's just a child. Nothing to be afraid of.'

Zac closed his eyes again, blocking out the memories, the pain. 'I'll think about it,' he said eventually.

'It's time for you to move on. Trust me, mate. Remember, I'm always right!'

## CHAPTER FIVE

'I's MORNING, Mummy,' Edward said the following Saturday morning, and Julia reached out and pulled him into bed with her.

'Morning, darling,' she said, her eyes still closed. He wriggled and squirmed into a comfortable position as Julia kissed his head and neck. 'Mmm, you're delicious, Edward.'

'No, I not. You 'licious, Mummy,' he said as he smothered her face with sloppy kisses.

She opened her eyes and peered at the clock. 'Six-thirty. Right on time. You're the best alarm clock and so cuddly to wake up to.'

He was still for a whole two seconds before wriggling again, sitting up and asking for a pillow fight.

Julia smiled at him and summoned some energy. She'd been called into Theatre just after one o'clock in the morning with a car accident victim. The patient would require extensive knee reconstruction but last night she'd merely cleaned up the wound and stabilised the fracture until she could book him onto her operating list for Tuesday.

She'd arrived home just before five and now that she had her sweet alarm clock hovering over her, pillow held firmly in his little arms, she knew there wasn't any hope of going back to sleep. At least, not now! She clutched the pillow behind her head and yanked it out, gently aiming it in his direction.

'Ugh. You dot me, Mum.' He fell onto the bed and giggled. 'I get you now, Mummy. I get you.' Edward brought his pillow down on top of her head and Julia laughed. 'I dot you, Mum.'

Julia aimed again and knocked him on the arm and then the leg. He came crashing down onto her, his knee going into her stomach. 'Ugh. Careful, mate. How did you get to be so bony?' she mumbled before his pillow came down on her again.

They played until Edward's attention wandered and he thought of something else to do.

'Go back to bed,' her mother said when she shuffled into the kitchen fifteen minutes later.

Julia smiled. 'I'm fine. It'll catch up with me later today.'

'Then make sure you rest. Are you still going out with Zac tonight?'

'He hasn't said anything but after his let's-be-friends speech earlier on in the week, I sincerely doubt it. Besides, we're both on call so who knows? We may end up spending the night together in Theatre.'

'I heard you come in not that long ago.' Cassandra made tea and handed Julia a cup.

'Perfect,' Julia said, and closed her eyes as she sipped the brew.

'What was it?'

Julia frowned and concentrated on her mother's words. 'Oh, the emergency?'

Her mother nodded. A retired nurse, Cassandra Bolton loved to talk about the medical side of her daughter's work.

'Comminuted fracture to the right patella. I just cleaned it up but it'll need reconstruction next week.'

'Any need to call Zac in?'

'No. Rodney, the registrar, and I coped quite well, thank you very much.'

'I wasn't implying that you couldn't, dear.'

'I know,' Julia said with a smile. 'It's just been one very busy week. I sincerely hope things settle down.'

'You just need to become comfortable with your new schedule, dear, then you'll be able to cope better.' Cassandra placed some jam and toast in front of Julia. 'Where's Edward?'

'Playing cars. Where else?'

'All boys like to play with cars.'

'And it doesn't change when they get older.'

'Yes, I saw Zac's car when he dropped you home on Thursday night after that surprise thunderstorm.'

'Boys and their toys,' Julia murmured as she ate her toast. She'd told him that she was quite willing to take a taxi but he'd insisted and as they were 'friends', she'd decided it couldn't do any harm.

'Did I tell you that Mona called last night?' Cassandra asked. Julia shook her head. 'Sorry. She and Jeffrey are coming around for lunch today so try and have your rest before then.'

'Yes, Mum,' Julia said in a soldier tone, and saluted.

'Don't get cheeky.'

'No, Mum,' she said in the same tone, and they both smiled.

For the rest of the morning, Julia relaxed and rested, dozing as she lay on the floor beside Edward who was playing with his building blocks.

They had a wonderful time with Mona and Jeffrey who brought a battery-operated car for Edward. Jeffrey and Edward proceeded to play with it for the next few hours, both 'boys' thoroughly enjoying themselves.

'You shouldn't spoil him so much,' Julia said to Mona.

'Oh, nonsense. We don't have any grandchildren yet and he's just so adorable, he simply begs to be spoilt. You know we count you as family. Besides, it gives Jeffrey a good excuse to revisit his childhood.'

Shortly after five o'clock, as they were saying goodbye to the McArthurs, Julia's mobile phone rang. 'Uh-oh. That's going to be the hospital, I can just feel it,' she said as she rushed inside to answer it.

'Dr Bolton.'

'Julia.' Zac's deep voice came through and Julia closed her eyes. She sank down into a chair. Friends or not, he still had the ability to affect her just by saying her name.

'Problem?' she asked.

'What gave you that idea?' he said with an ironic laugh, but went on before she could answer. 'Yes, as a matter of fact. Two hotshots from a karate competition have both sustained injuries to their hands. They're in X-Ray at the moment, but if you come in then we can get them both sorted out tonight.'

'OK. I'll leave now. See you soon.'

While Zac waited for Julia to arrive, he walked up to his office in the department and started to sort through some paperwork. The top sheet on his 'to be done' pile was a request from one of his registrars asking Zac to give a reference for his application to a hospital in a Third World country.

'No.' Zac shook his head and put the piece of paper aside, deciding to think about the request later. He picked up another piece of paper and dictated a reply, but his gaze kept returning to the first piece. 'Don't do it, mate,' he said softly. After Zac's own time spent in the Third World, years ago, he wondered whether these doctors *really* knew what they were letting themselves in for.

He dictated another letter and once more came back to the first request. He placed his elbows onto the desk and buried his head in his hands as the memories started to swamp him again.

His time overseas had been good to start with. Until he'd been moved to an emergency hospital that had been overcrowded and desperately needed his services. There he'd met Cara. It had been over three years since her death and an image of her beautiful smiling face appeared in his mind.

'No,' he said again, his jaw clenched. The hurt, the anxiety and the pain all came flooding back, and hard on its heels were the memories of Zoe. His darling daughter, Zoe. So small and so fragile. She'd fitted into the palm of his hand, the hand that now held his head in anguish.

He opened up a drawer and took out some paracetamol. He swallowed them down without water and stood from his desk. He glared down at the offensive piece of paper that had started this train of thought. If he'd known it was going to be there, he wouldn't have come up here—not alone in the department on the weekend when there was no noise around to distract him and help keep his thoughts on track.

He scribbled a note on a sticky memo pad and stuck it to the request before tossing it into his out-basket. If that very competent registrar wanted a reference, Zac wanted to talk with him face to face first to ensure he knew exactly what he was up against.

Zac walked to the door, deciding to return to A and E where there was at least a bit of noise to help drive away the intrusive thoughts. War zones weren't good places to work in, and of *that* he had first-hand knowledge. There had been days when Zac hadn't been sure whether or not he'd live to see the next sunrise.

He pushed open the door to A and E and looked around for Julia. Surely she was here by now.

'Ah, Julia,' he said as he walked into the tearoom. 'You're here. Perfect timing. You've saved me from some paperwork.'

'Ugh. Anything but paperwork.'

Zac laughed, trying not to notice how his entire mood had picked up at the mere sight of her. She was gorgeous, even though she looked exhausted.

'What's happening with the patients?' she asked.

'I don't know. Why don't we go and see the triage sister?'

'They're held up in Radiology,' Sister explained. 'One of the processing machines has broken down. Shouldn't be too much longer.'

'Let us know when you're ready,' Zac said. 'We'll be in the tearoom.' They returned to the tearoom.

'Why don't you tell me what you know about the patients?' Julia asked.

'All right. They're both nineteen, both competing in the same karate competition this afternoon. First patient is Lucas Carter. He was attempting to break seven tiles and sustained a hand injury. Then Philip Gregg attempted the same feat and *also* sustained a hand injury.'

Julia raised her eyebrows in surprise, her lips twitching with amusement. 'Did either of them win?'

'I don't know. We'll have to ask them.' Zac matched Julia's smile and for a split second she knew that being friends would definitely work—for now. It was controlling their animalistic attraction to each other that would require restraint!

The atmosphere around them started to grow with intensity. Zac was so handsome and the way he was smiling at her now turned her insides to mush. She cleared her throat nervously and licked her lips.

'Right. I might go and get changed into theatre scrubs.'

She had to get away from him—get control of her emotions.

Zac raised his eyebrows, the smile still on his lips. 'You've always looked gorgeous in baggy green cotton.'

'Why, thank you, Dr Carmichael.' She matched his teasing mood. 'You say the sweetest things.' Julia turned and headed towards the changing rooms. The truth was that his teasing smile had caused her heart rate to increase and her palms to sweat. Would she ever get used to the effect Zachary Carmichael had on her? She doubted it.

After she had changed, Julia went to Emergency Theatres to check and double-check the instrumentation. Just as she was finishing, her pager sounded. She checked the message. It was from her mother, asking her to call home. She checked the clock. Five-thirty. Edward would be getting ready for his bath and, no doubt, kicking up a fuss.

She didn't know where the phones were around the A and E department so went into the tearoom where she'd seen a phone earlier. She dialled an outside line before punching in her number. 'Hi, it's me,' she said, and could hear her son wailing in the background. 'What's wrong?' She couldn't hide the instant alarm that sprang into her tone.

'He's all right,' her mother said. 'He's just very tired and wants you.'

'Put him on,' she said, and took a deep breath.

'Mummy,' Edward sniffled. 'I want Mummy,' he said stubbornly.

'Hi, sweetie. What's wrong, darling?'

'I want *you*, Mummy. I want *you*.'

'Oh, honey, I know,' she said, feeling for him. This was the part of her job that she hated. The part that took her away from her boy! 'Mummy has to go and help some sick people. You be a good boy for Grandma and go to sleep, and then in the morning you can come and wake me up and we'll have a really, really *big* pillow fight. How does that sound?'

'An' play I pie?' he asked.

'Yes,' she promised with a smile. 'We'll play I Spy as well.'

'Oh-tay,' he said, still sad, but at least his crying had stopped.

'Good. I love you, darling.'

'I love you, too, Mummy,' he said, and blew a big kiss down the receiver. Julia waited a moment before her mother came back on the line.

'Thanks. He just needed to hear your voice.'

'I know. I'll be home as soon as I can.'

'All right, dear. Bye.'

'Bye,' she said softly, and hung up. Julia sighed and shook her head before turning around. She froze when she spotted Zac leaning against the doorframe, his face concerned.

'Everything all right?'

'Yes.' She nodded for emphasis. 'That was my mother.' She pointed to the phone. 'Edward's a little overtired. Jeffrey and Mona came for lunch today and brought a new remote-control car for him. He always gets over-excited when Jeffrey comes.' Julia smiled, her tone not in the least severe or reproving.

'That doesn't bother you?'

'*Someone* has to get him over-excited about boy things like cars. Mummy and Grandma don't know diddly-squat about them.'

'Oh, you don't do too bad. You surely impressed young Timmy on the ward last week.'

'I've figured out how to tell one car from another. The name and make are written underneath them.'

'Ah, so that's your secret.'

Julia was amazed that Zac was standing there, talking to her about her son. Every other time she'd mentioned Edward during the week she'd received 'the mask' from him. Now he seemed...interested.

'So a few words from Mummy and he's as right as rain, eh?'

Julia smiled. 'Something like that.'

He hesitated and Julia held her breath. He was about to say something important and she didn't want to put him off.

'Vanessa gets back in a few days' time,' he said conversationally.

'Oh. Have you spoken to her?'

He nodded. 'Last night. When I told her you were here, she was so excited she squealed down the phone. She hasn't done that since she was a teenager. My ear is still recovering,' he jested, rubbing the ear in question.

Julia laughed. 'Sounds like Vanessa.'

'Anyway, as next weekend is our weekend off, she suggested we drive to their place in Brisbane and stay for the night.'

Julia's smile slowly turned into a polite one. 'Thanks for the offer, Zac, but I couldn't possibly—'

'Not just you, Julia. Edward and your mother are invited as well,' he clarified.

'Oh.' She was surprised but then reasoned that Vanessa *would* invite the whole family. 'All right, then. I'll talk it over with Mum and see what she says. She might actually be glad to have a weekend away.'

'Good. Let me know, then.'

Theatre Sister stopped in the tearoom doorway. 'There you both are. The patients are back,' she informed them.

'Thanks.' Zac turned to Julia. 'You take Lucas, I'll take Philip and let's see if we can't get out of here sooner rather than later.'

Julia nodded as they both headed over to their patients.

'Hi, Lucas. I'm Dr Bolton,' Julia said as she entered treatment room one. 'Sounds as though you've had quite a night,' she ventured, but Lucas just sulked. Fair enough, she thought as she switched on a lamp by the bed and angled it so she could get a closer look at Lucas's hand. The nurse who was attending to Lucas held out the casenotes to Julia. She read them quickly before crossing to the sink to wash her hands.

'All right, now,' she said as she dried her hands and pulled on a pair of gloves. 'Let's take a look at your radiographs and see what's going on.' Julia took the X-rays out of the packet and held them up to the light.

'Have a look here,' she said to Lucas, but he simply turned his head away.

'No.'

'OK. Well, these X-rays show me that the fourth and fifth metacarpals—they're the bones on top of your hand— are broken as well as all three sections of the fourth and fifth phalanges—they're your fingers.' As she was talking, she saw Lucas's head shift slightly so she pointed to the bones in question.

Julia lowered the films and placed them back in the packet. 'Now, if I can just have a look at your fingers, we'll be all done.'

'Why can't you just read the ambulance report and be done with it?' Lucas demanded, still cradling his injured hand in his good one. 'They've already poked and prodded it. Said I broke a couple of fingers. Then I had those

X-ray people touchin' me. I'm just fed up with everything,' he said, his voice cracking slightly.

Julia remained silent, hoping he'd continue. It was better for him to get things out in the open rather than bottling them up.

'If I made it through this round, I was going to Brisbane for the finals. Now I'm out of it. At least *Philip* didn't win.' His voice was laced with bad sportsmanship and Julia now had the answer to her earlier question. *Neither* of them had won.

She could understand Lucas's sour-grapes attitude but at the moment she didn't have a lot of reserved patience for dealing with him. After being called to the hospital last night, spending an exhausting day with her son and now having to tread carefully with her uncooperative patient, Julia had just about had enough. Still, she was a professional.

'I realise you're not feeling up to this, Lucas, and I know the paramedics have already poked and prodded you but I'm sorry to tell you it doesn't end there. Lucas, I'm the surgeon who's going to be treating you, and just by reading their report and looking at the X-rays I can already tell that you're going to need surgery. Now, as I'll be the person performing the surgery, I think it's best if I can have a good look at them so I know exactly what I have to fix.' Her speech was delivered quietly and calmly and she waited for Lucas to digest her words.

'All right, then,' he said reluctantly.

Julia reached out and drew his arm closer to her. 'Thank you,' she replied. She gently tested the range of motion, only to have Lucas yell out in pain.

'That hurts. That's enough.' He snatched his hand back.

'Thank you.' She'd seen enough for the moment. She turned her attention to the paperwork the nurse had set out for her and after writing her comments she said, 'I'll see you after your pre-med.'

Returning to the tearoom, she encountered Zac. 'Fourth and fifth metacarpals and phalanges?' he asked, and she nodded.

He chuckled and shook his head. 'Exactly the same injury.'

'And neither of them won.'

'Actually, Philip didn't say. He was just glad his hand is going to be all right. He said he'd only taken up the sport for a bit of fun and this would be another story he could tell his grandchildren.'

'Sounds as though you have the patient from heaven.'

'Why? You don't?' Zac smiled at her.

'You could say that. Hopefully Lucas will have a better outlook once he's had the surgery and is on the road to recovery.' Julia dropped wearily into a chair at the table and slumped forward. 'A difficult patient is the last thing I need right now. I'm just so tired,' she moaned to herself.

'What?'

She raised her head and looked at him. 'I'm tired, Zac. I was in Theatre early this morning, didn't get home until just after five and then Edward woke me up at six-thirty.' She buried her head in her hands and mumbled, 'I know I just need to find my pace but, with moving across the country, starting a new job and trying to get Edward settled into a routine again, it's all very draining.'

'I think I caught most of that,' she heard Zac say from behind her, and jerked her head upright when she felt the warm pressure of his hands on her shoulders. 'Try and relax,' he said softly. 'At least for a few minutes.'

Julia sat up a bit straighter to allow his massaging hands access to her shoulders. She closed her eyes. 'Mmm,' she groaned, and breathed in deeply. 'I remember those magic hands.' Two seconds after the words were out, she tensed again and opened her eyes. 'I mean, you've always been good at massaging,' she corrected, just in case he should interpret her words another way. 'Shoulders,' she added quickly. 'Massaging shoulders.'

His deep chuckle washed over her with delight. 'I know what you meant, Julia. Now, help me out by relaxing so I can try and unknot your shoulders with my magic hands.'

Julia smiled at his words, closed her eyes and tried hard to relax—which was easier said than done as whenever Zac touched her, her entire body came to life. She tried hard not to focus on the warmth of his fingers, she tried hard not to focus on his close proximity, she tried hard not to focus on the scent of his cologne, but rather on how he was easing the tension in her shoulders. It wasn't easy but slowly she managed it, and as Zac's hands continued to move in rhythmic strokes over her shoulders and neck, Julia slowly felt the tension start to ease out of her.

'How does that feel?'

The question was whispered close to her ear as his deep voice rumbled through her. Julia's eyes snapped open and she shivered involuntarily.

Slowly she turned her head to look at him and was amazed to read desire in his blue eyes. 'Zac?' she whispered, her lips parting as her breathing increased. They stared at each other for one heart-stopping moment before Zac pressed his mouth firmly to her own.

Julia sighed into the kiss as their lips met with a burning mutual need. Her blood was pumping furiously around her body, zinging with excitement as Zac's tongue slipped between her lips. She matched the intensity of his passion, giving everything she had to the man she was falling for all over again.

He groaned and hoisted her out of the chair and into his

arms in one swift movement. Julia heard the chair hit the ground behind her but couldn't be bothered picking it up. She was caught up in the charm that was Zachary Carmichael. The way he made her feel, the way she hoped she made *him* feel. It was too powerful to ignore yet that's what they'd both been trying to do.

She allowed her fingers the luxury of sinking themselves into his hair, ensuring that he wasn't about to break the sweet torture his mouth was evoking on her senses. She gave all of herself to the kiss, letting him know how much she'd missed this more intimate contact and how much she loved it. She was simply enjoying being in Zac's arms, with his mouth on hers, his body pressed close. Eventually she pulled back, her breathing erratic as she gasped for air. He kissed her briefly a few more times before she rested her head against his chest. 'Baggy green cotton will do it every time,' she jested, referring to his earlier remark about the theatre garb they were both wearing.

Zac chuckled and she rejoiced at the sound. Taking a deep breath, her pulse slowly returned to normal and almost reluctantly Zac let her go. She slid her arms from around him and hugged herself tightly, feeling deprived. 'We should really be more careful.' He pointed to the open tearoom door.

What did that imply? That they were going to continue kissing but it should be done in private? Julia shook her head. No. If they were going to be just *friends* then they shouldn't be kissing at all!

Should she remind him of that? Julia glanced surreptitiously up at Zac to see him run a not-so-steady hand through his hair.

'You know, Zac...' Julia hesitated for a moment but decided it was best to continue with what she'd been about to say. One of them would say it and she would rather it was her. 'It's going to take every ounce of strength from both of us to make this friendship thing work.'

He nodded, rubbing his hand along the back of his neck. 'You're right.' He smiled crookedly and shrugged his shoulders. 'There just seem to be times when I find it impossible to keep my hands off you.'

'Ditto,' she agreed, noticing the flash of desire in his eyes again. 'Inner strength. We both need to find some.'

He chuckled without humour. 'It won't be easy.'

'No,' she agreed. 'It won't but, nevertheless, we're two professionals who work well together and should be able to deal with seeing each other socially—'

'Without succumbing to the temptation to be in each other's arms,' he finished.

They both nodded again. Their gazes locked, sending underlying messages of suppressed passion. Zac cleared his throat and looked away.

'I'm sorry I kissed you, Julia. I do like you, but we can only be friends. Happy families aren't for me. I won't go through it again.'

Julia frowned. '*Again?*' she whispered, as she instinctively took a step away from him. What was he talking about? Another step and... Julia found herself falling backwards, the legs of the upended chair digging into her.

'Whoa!' She tumbled over, arms and legs flailing in the air before her arm connected with the side of the chair and her backside with the floor. 'Ouch!' she groaned, and winced in pain.

'Jules, are you all right?' Zac was instantly by her side, helping her to her feet, his previous defensiveness gone. 'Julia?'

'Ugh,' she complained as she rubbed the side of her arm. 'I'm so embarrassed.'

'Hey—it's just *me*. No need to be embarrassed.' He held

her arm tenderly and rubbed his thumb over the red mark that was beginning to appear.

'It's...f-fine.' Julia took a step away from him. Moments ago he'd been wanting to keep his distance simply because she had a child.

'Let me move this out of the way,' he said as he picked up the chair and returned it to the table. 'There you go. That nasty chair won't hurt you again, Jules.'

She smiled at his teasing and then grimaced again as she moved. 'My...hero,' she said stiltedly. 'Now, if you'll excuse me, I think I'll adjourn to the female changing rooms where I can gather the remnants of my dignity in private.'

Zac stepped back and swept his arm out wide in a gallant gesture. 'As you wish,' he said, trying to raise a smile. He succeeded. 'I'll go and check on our patients.'

Julia preceded him out of the tearoom and headed to the female changing rooms without giving him a backward glance. She carefully sat down on the bench near her locker and hung her head, slowly stretching her neck and spine. 'Ouch,' she whimpered again. Looking down at the angry red mark across her forearm, she gave it another rub.

Then she became aware of a dull ache across her back and at the base of her spine. She gently stood up and walked to the full-length mirror attached to the wall. Lifting the back of her theatre shirt, she twisted slightly to look at her back. Sure enough, a matching angry red mark was found.

Giving it a rub as well, she lowered her top and headed for the door. 'Ooh,' she said, and winced as she walked. 'I think a trip to the hospital pharmacy might be in order,' she mumbled as she left the changing rooms.

'I was wondering when you were going to resurface,'

Zac said as he lounged against the wall, obviously waiting for her.

'Problem?' She schooled her features so they didn't show her pain.

'No.'

'Good.' She started to walk up the corridor but stopped and winced.

'You *did* hurt yourself.' He nodded knowingly. 'I thought so. Where does it hurt?'

'I think I've bruised my coccyx,' she told him and shook her head in annoyance.

'Ouch,' he said sympathetically. 'I did that in my last year of med school, remember?'

'Yes, but at least you didn't fall over a chair. You bruised yours honourably.'

'I'd hardly call getting tackled in a rugby scrum honourable but I know what you mean.' His smile was back in place as he tenderly placed his arm about her waist. 'Let's get you back to the tearoom and I'll go down to the pharmacy and get some anti-inflammatories for you. We'll fill out the paperwork for Occupational Health and Safety later.'

'Zac, I—'

'Don't argue with me, Jules. Doctor's orders,' he said pointedly as they reached the tearoom. 'Now be careful of the chair,' he joked. 'I don't want it to attack you again.'

'Ha, ha,' she said dryly, but allowed him to help her to sit down. She made sure she was sitting slightly forward rather than slouching back, which would have put pressure on her spine and bruised coccyx.

Within no time at all he was back, carrying a small bottle of tablets in one hand and some sandwiches from a vending machine in the other. He put everything down on the table and walked to the sink to get a glass of water.

The tablets were a non-steroidal anti-inflammatory drug which she'd prescribed thousands of times for her own patients.

'I want you to take two anti-inflammatories now to help with the pain. Before bed tonight, I want you to take two more.' He started to unwrap the sandwiches. 'Make sure you persist with the course for at least the next week and, yes, Julia, I *will* be checking up on you.'

'Oh, great,' she mumbled without enthusiasm.

He held out a sandwich to her. 'Eat.'

'You have got to be joking. I never eat vending machine food.'

'Stop being difficult, Julia. You know you need to take anti-inflammatories with food, so take a bite.'

Julia looked at the sandwich with distaste. 'There weren't any apples in the vending machine?' she queried.

'Julia!'

'Oh, all right,' she snapped. She gave in with reluctance and took the sandwich from him. She was feeling useless and vulnerable and although she didn't like Zac to see her like this, she was glad it was him and no one else.

'Eat all of that half, please.'

Her only reply was to take another bite. When she'd finished, he shook out two tablets and handed them to her, watching her swallow them with the water.

'What a good girl. I'm glad you're being so co-operative.'

'Only because I have to,' she sulked, and he laughed.

'Come on, it's not that bad.'

She sighed. 'You're right.'

He sat down next to her and gave her hand a reassuring squeeze before letting go. Both of them were quiet for a while before Julia broke the silence.

'Thanks for taking care of me. It's been a long time

since you've nursed me, Zac, and all I can say is that your bedside manner still needs attending to. Still as brisk and blunt as ever.' She took another sip of the water, eyeing the other half of the sandwich with distaste. At least he wasn't going to make her eat that half as well.

He frowned at her. 'When did I...?' He stopped, gazing off into the distance. 'That's right.' He snapped his fingers in remembrance. 'When that awful flu virus did the rounds of the med school. I nursed you and then you nursed me. I'd forgotten all about it.'

'All I know is it took you ages to recover.'

'Garbage. Just because you heal miraculously overnight, it doesn't mean you should pick on others whose bodies take a more leisurely rate to heal.'

'Zac, it was almost two weeks that you were down. I was down for three days!'

'Did you ever think I might have been faking it?' He wiggled his eyebrows up and down. 'Perhaps the thought of you coming to care for me every day was more exciting than admitting I was better.'

'Were you?' she asked.

His smile grew wide and his eyes twinkled with mischief, but he didn't confirm or deny it.

'What if I *knew* you were faking near the end and decided I *liked* nursing you?'

He laughed. 'I'd say we're two of a kind.'

For the umpteenth time in the past few hours Julia found herself gazing into his eyes, working hard to resist the magnetic pull that existed between them.

# CHAPTER SIX

'YOUR patients are ready,' the A and E sister said as she poked her head around the open tearoom doorway. She looked from one to the other and then noticed the medicine on the table. 'Everything all right?'

'Fine,' Zac responded. 'Dr Bolton had a slight altercation with a chair.'

Sister's lips twitched. 'Who won?'

'The chair,' Julia said with disgust as she braced her hands on the table to help herself stand.

'Will you be all right for Theatre?' Sister asked.

'I'll be fine.' Julia brushed away the concern. 'I'm just feeling a bit stiff at the moment and there's nothing like a good operating session to really help the kinks set in.'

Sister laughed and headed off. Julia could feel Zac watching her closely. He crossed to her side and placed his hand beneath her elbow for support.

'Are you sure?' he asked seriously.

'I'll be fine, Zac,' she reiterated. 'After all, I have the great Zachary Carmichael looking after me.'

She and Zac went into separate theatres at the same time and Julia found that once she got going she was fine. She also knew the anti-inflammatories Zac had made her take would definitely help to dull the pain. Bruised coccyx bones were annoyingly painful and healed very slowly. At least in Theatre, once she was in position, she didn't have to move much.

Lucas Carter's hand required open reduction and internal fixation with K-wires, and an hour after she'd started

# GET A FREE TEDDY BEAR...

You'll love this adorable bear with its little waistcoat and bow-tie in royal blue felt. Measuring approximately 140mm, he has moveable arms and legs and is sure to delight everybody who sees him. And he's yours FREE when you accept this no-risk offer!

# AND TWO FREE BOOKS!

Here's the chance to get two Mills & Boon® novels from the Medical Romance™ series **absolutely free!** These books have a retail value of £2.55.

There's no catch. You're under no obligation to buy anything. We charge nothing – ZERO – for your first shipment. And you don't have to make any minimum number of purchases – not even one!

Find out for yourself why thousands of readers enjoy receiving books by post from the Reader Service™. They like the convenience of home delivery... they like getting the best new novels before they are available in the shops... and they love the fact that **postage and packing is entirely free!** Why not try us and see! Return this card promptly. You don't even need a stamp!

**YES!** Please send me two free Medical Romance™ novels and my free Teddy Bear. I understand that I am under no obligation to purchase any books, as explained overleaf. I am over 18 years of age.

M2CI

MS/MRS/MISS/MR _____ INITIALS _____

BLOCK CAPITALS PLEASE

SURNAME _____

ADDRESS _____

_____

POSTCODE _____

Offer valid in the UK only and is not available to current Reader Service subscribers to the Medical Romance series. Overseas and Eire please write for details. We reserve the right to refuse an application and applicants must be 18 years of age or over. Only one application per household. Offer expires 31st October 2002. As a result of this application, you may be mailed with further offers from other carefully selected companies. If you would prefer not to share in this opportunity please write to The Data Manager at the address shown overleaf.

Mills & Boon® is a registered trademark owned by Harlequin Mills & Boon Limited.
Medical Romance™ is being used as a trademark.

# NO OBLIGATION TO BUY!

## THE READER SERVICE™ : HERE'S HOW IT WORKS

Accepting the free books and gift places you under no obligation to buy anything. You may keep the books and gift and return the despatch note marked 'cancel'. If we do not hear from you, about a month later we will send you 4 more books and invoice you just £2.55* each. That's the complete price – there is no extra charge for postage and packing. You may cancel at any time, otherwise every month we'll send you 4 more books, which you may either purchase or return – the choice is yours.

*Terms and prices subject to change without notice.

**NO STAMP NEEDED!**

**THE READER SERVICE™**
**FREEPOST CN81**
**CROYDON**
**SURREY**
**CR9 3WZ**

**YOURS FREE!**

NO STAMP NEEDED IF POSTED IN THE U.K. OR N.I.

Julia was ready to close. Thankfully, the surgery had been straightforward with no complications.

When Julia came out, she headed straight for the changing rooms. The sooner she was at home in bed, the better. After changing, Julia went to Recovery to check on Lucas and also to see if Philip was there. Zac had still been in Theatre when she'd finished and she hoped he hadn't run into any problems.

Both patients were there and Zac was standing at the nurses' station, already changed, talking quietly with the nursing staff. Julia checked on Lucas before sauntering carefully over to where Zac stood.

'Feeling stiff?' he asked.

'A little.' She nodded.

'You poor thing,' one of the nurses said, oozing sympathy. 'I bruised my coccyx in high school and it still gives me trouble sometimes.'

'I see Dr Carmichael has been spreading hospital gossip!' She glared at him but he just smiled and shrugged.

'We all seem to bruise our coccyx bones at some point in our lives,' agreed another nurse.

'Thanks,' Julia responded with a forced smile.

'Well, ladies.' Zac reached into his trouser pocket and pulled out his car keys. 'We'll leave you to it. If you have any problems you know our numbers. Right now I'm going to walk Julia out to her car to make sure she gets there in one piece.' He chuckled and the nurses joined in, the sympathetic looks returning as they all looked at Julia.

As they headed outside, Zac's arm beneath her elbow for support, Julia felt goose-bumps cascade over her body. Was it from the rain that was softly falling or Zac's touch?

'So nice of you to share my misfortune with the rest of the hospital,' she quipped.

'No need to thank me. It was nothing.'

'Zac! I sincerely hope you didn't tell them how I did it?'

'I told them you'd had a disagreement with a chair.'

'Zac!' she spluttered again. 'It was embarrassing enough that it happened in front of you or should I say *because* of you. If I hadn't been fighting the need to kiss you again, I wouldn't have tripped over the darn thing in the first place.'

'So it's all my fault?'

'Correct, and you'd better not forget it,' she said crossly.

'Where's your car?' Zac asked, changing the subject, and Julia pointed to the white sedan parked next to his Jag. 'Good. Give me your keys, please.'

'Why?' Julia held them tightly in her hand.

'I'm driving you home, that's why.'

'Zac,' she protested. 'I'm more than capable of—'

'Do you want to stand and argue in the rain?'

'Well, what if I do?' she demanded.

He smiled at her. 'Julia, you can't be feeling all that good after the operating session. I'd rather you didn't have a car accident on the way home and therefore I intend to drive you home, walk back to the hospital and then collect my own car.'

'Then it looks as though you're going to get *really* wet,' she retorted, and crossed her arms defensively. 'Which means we can stand here and argue the point for as long as it takes. I don't need you to drive me anywhere, Zac.' Julia had had enough and just wanted to go home—alone.

'You are the most stubborn woman I've ever met.' He shook his head. 'Fine, then. You drive but I'll follow you in my car to make sure you get there safely.'

'Fine.' Julia unlocked her car and watched as Zac did the same to his. 'It might be a new experience for you—

being forced to stick to the speed limit for a change,' she called as she carefully lowered herself into the car.

'I'm not going to dignify that with a response.' He shut his door and started the engine.

As Julia adjusted herself in the driver's seat, she reluctantly admitted that perhaps Zac had been right. She was in pain but, she rationalised as she clipped the seat belt in, she'd been through worse. Giving birth to Edward had been the most painful experience of her life as she'd had no time for an epidural, and she now equated all pain against that one event. This was a cinch in comparison!

Sure enough, Zac followed her all the way home. After she'd garaged the car, she stayed in it, wondering how on earth she was going to get out. She undid her seat belt and opened the door. Trying to shift one leg had her crying out in agony.

'Will you let me help you now?' Zac looked down at her through the open door.

'I guess I'll have to,' she replied. 'Either that or sleep the whole night in the car.' She tried to laugh but it came out as a whimper.

'Which won't do you any good at all. Right,' he said, and crouched down to slip his arms beneath her shoulders and ever so gently lift her out. Julia winced and grimaced, trying to hide the pain from Zac.

'House keys,' he ordered after he'd locked her car and garage. Julia handed them over without fuss and took the opportunity to lean on him as he helped her inside. He smelled good, he felt good—he was good.

'I feel so useless,' she muttered.

'It'll ease in a day or two,' he said softly as he closed the front door behind him and dropped her keys on the hall table. The clock on the wall said it was half past seven. At least she knew that Edward was asleep. Her son was usually safely in dreamland by a quarter to seven—which was why he was always awake at what seemed like the crack of dawn. 'Which one is your room?' he whispered.

'Oh, Mum can settle me,' Julia protested, but Zac simply shook his head.

'You are going straight to bed. Do not pass Go, do not collect two hundred dollars.'

'End of the hall,' she muttered, as they made their way up the corridor. She felt a little uncomfortable, heading to her bedroom with a man. Not just *any* man, she corrected herself, but *Zac*! Even though there was nothing...romantic about it, it still felt strange.

After he'd opened the door and helped her over to the queen-sized bed in the middle of the room, Zac slowly eased away.

'I'm going to get you a glass of water and some food so you can take another dose of the anti-inflammatories. Can you manage to undress by yourself or would you like some help?' There was nothing leering or suggestive in his tone and she realised Zac had switched into 'doctor' mode.

'Ask Mum to come and help me, please,' she said, and he nodded before leaving the room. Moments later her door opened again and her mother walked in.

'Oh, darling, are you all right? Zac just told me what happened.'

Julia sat very still as she unbuttoned her shirt, wincing when her mother sat down on the bed beside her. 'Oh, Mum,' she whimpered. 'It was a ridiculous accident but I've bruised my coccyx.'

'So he said. You poor dear,' Cassandra said in sympathy as she slowly stood, being careful not to rock the bed. 'Let's get you ready for a long, healing sleep and hopefully you'll feel better in a day or two.'

By the time Zac knocked on her bedroom door, opening

it without waiting for a reply, Julia was changed and beneath the cotton sheet on her bed. 'How's the patient, Mrs Bolton?'

'Oh, for heaven's sake, Zac, call me Cassandra.' She motioned to the sandwich and glass of water he carried. 'Anti-inflammatories?'

He nodded and looked at Julia, a small smile on his lips. 'Where are they, Jules?'

'In my bag.' Julia pointed to where she'd dumped her bag at the end of her bed.

Without asking, he went through her bag, found the tablets and handed them over to Cassandra. 'Two tablets, twice a day with food. Make sure she takes them, please.' Zac transferred his gaze from Cassandra to Julia.

'I'll make sure she does. Julia was always a terrible patient as a child. A trait she inherited from me, I think.'

Zac's smile increased. 'Give her another dose now to help her sleep,' he said, as though Julia wasn't in the room. She fumed inwardly as he turned to look at her. 'The sandwich is peanut butter, which I hope you still like.'

Julia nodded. 'And made with fresh bread,' she said, eyeing the sandwich he handed her. 'Much better than your previous offering.'

He chuckled. 'Thank you. Well, I'll leave you in Cassandra's capable hands. Get some sleep.' Zac stared longingly at Julia for a moment before turning and leaving. Cassandra started to follow him. 'No, don't bother, Cassandra. I'll see myself out. You...' he pointed to Julia '...take it easy tomorrow and I'll see you on Monday.'

She nodded again and watched him leave her room.

'My goodness me,' Cassandra whispered after they'd heard the front door shut. 'The tension between the two of you is so palpable. I wish you'd do something about it, dear.'

'Mum—this really isn't the time.'

'No, I don't suppose it is.'

The sound of Edward coughing made them both stop for a moment. 'I'll check on him,' Cassandra said. 'Finish your sandwich.'

'Yes, Mum.' When her mother left the room, Julia closed her eyes as she ate, reflecting on the night's events. What didn't Zac want to go through *again*? Was it a relationship with her? There was no denying that the old spark still existed. Had their break-up ten years ago been as painful for him as it had been for her?

Julia finished the sandwich and thought about her life during the past decade. No. She shook her head. She'd never fully recovered from her break-up with Zac but surely now it was worth giving it another go?

'Friends,' she whispered softly into the still room. She knew Edward had been a deciding factor in Zac suggesting they become friends but maybe after spending some time together—just as friends—hopefully Zac would begin to see what a wonderful boy Edward was. He was adorable, gorgeous, polite and energetic. Then again, perhaps she had a biased opinion of her son. Julia smiled to herself as she swallowed her tablets down.

'Is he all right?' she asked when her mother came back into her room. She had something in her hands and placed a little bell on Julia's bedside table.

'He's fine. I think he had a little pain in his tummy so I rubbed his back and he's settled again.' Cassandra picked up the empty plate and glass. 'All done?'

Julia nodded.

'Right, then, I think it's time we all got some rest. Ring the bell if you need help getting up to go to the bathroom.'

'Mum, I—'

'You're as stubborn as I am, Julia Louise Bolton. Now,

do as you're told. I don't want you aggravating your back any more than necessary. Understood?'

'Yes, Mum,' Julia replied obediently.

Her mother plumped her pillows and helped her to wriggle down in the bed before kissing her forehead and leaving the room. Julia closed her eyes, feeling very much like a little girl instead of a thirty-three-year-old woman who held a surgical degree and was the mother of one.

Julia stayed in bed for most of Sunday, wincing when Edward came and jumped up and down on her mattress, demanding a pillow fight. He'd also insisted on kissing Mummy's back better and couldn't understand why it wasn't immediately as right as rain. The sentiment, however, made Julia love him all the more, if that was possible.

On Monday, she was definitely feeling better. Zac commented on it quietly during ward round.

'Range of motion seems to have increased,' he whispered as they walked between patients. Julia elbowed him sharply. 'Temper seems to be intact,' he continued, and she smiled. Tess, the ward sister, noticed the action and frowned at Julia. There was nothing for her to do but smile back as though nothing out of the ordinary was happening.

When they came to their karate experts, Lucas Carter and Philip Gregg, Julia was once again surprised at the difference in their personalities. Philip was as cheerful and optimistic as could be. His check X-ray, taken the night before, showed good stabilisation.

'You've had no after-effects from the anaesthetic,' Zac said as he read Philip's chart, 'so I don't see why you can't go home this morning.'

'All right!' Philip said, and grinned. 'Thanks, Dr Carmichael.'

'I'll see you in my clinic in two weeks' time,' he replied

and signed the patient's case-notes with the discharge details.

Lucas Carter was a different story. His check X-ray showed that everything was in the right place and only time would tell how well he would heal. But where Philip was full of optimism, Lucas was sunk in pessimism.

He was still rather sluggish, even though it had been almost thirty-seven hours since he'd come out of Theatre. It was a fact that general anaesthetics affected different people in different ways and Lucas was taking longer than usual to recover.

'When can I go home?' he asked Julia.

She checked his chart. 'I'd like you to stay in until at least this afternoon and have another course of antibiotics.'

Lucas sneered across at Philip who was in the next bed. 'How come he can go home and I can't?' he protested.

'Because you're not him.' Julia answered calmly. 'I'd like you to have another blood test and I'll check up on you later today.' She wrote up her request and they were about to move on to the next bed when Lucas erupted.

'Why didn't I get the male doctor? Why was I stuck with you? Females! Think they know everything. If I'd had him...' Lucas stabbed his finger in Zac's direction '...instead of *you*...' he pointed to Julia '...*I'd* be the one going home today and not *him*.' He glared at Philip as though he despised him, and Julia found it difficult to fathom just why Lucas didn't like Philip.

Zac stepped forward and the rest of the ward round, which was made up of registrars, interns, medical students and nursing staff, edged back a little. Julia calmly put her hand on Zac's arm and shook her head.

'I'm sorry you feel that way, Lucas,' she said quietly. 'If it makes you feel any better, I'm more than happy to hand your care over to Dr Carmichael here.' She waited for Lucas's reply. He seemed stunned. The entire ward round was silent, as were the other patients in the ward. The clock ticked for an entire five seconds without a sound.

Slowly Lucas lifted his chin in defiance, his eyes squinting with dislike for Julia. 'Yeah,' he said, and nodded for emphasis. 'Yeah. I want *him* to be my doctor.'

Julia picked up Lucas's chart, wrote the details and signed her name before handing the chart to Zac. He added his comments and, just like that, Lucas had a new doctor.

'Done,' she said, and smiled sweetly at him.

Zac looked at Lucas, his expression one of the consummate professional. 'I'd like to prescribe another course of antibiotics and I'll be around to see you later this afternoon,' he told Lucas, before replacing the chart and nodding to Julia. She was hard-pressed not to laugh at the look on Lucas's face.

'Shall we move on?' she asked the round, and everyone nodded or murmured affirmative replies.

They moved into the next ward which contained another six beds of male patients and where Aki Ishimaru had been transferred late last week. His asthma had been stabilised but Julia sensed there was still something wrong. His face was drawn and he looked very unhappy. She mentioned it to Zac, who agreed. When the round was finished, the two of them stayed at the nurses' station, discussing Aki's situation.

'Have we checked his diet? Is the food being prepared the correct way?' she asked.

'His notes say he's eating well.'

'Has he seen any of his friends? People from the tour bus?'

'Tess told me the other day that he refuses to.'

'I know he speaks very little English—maybe that's the

problem. How often does the translator come around to help the nursing staff?'

'Once a day.'

'Is it possible to make it twice?'

'More conversation? I'll ask Tess. Perhaps we should also schedule some extra times with the translator and social worker.'

'He doesn't want to see one,' Tess said as she came into the nurses' station. 'You're talking about Aki, aren't you?'

'Yes,' Julia answered.

'He doesn't want to see the social worker.'

'Why not?' Zac asked.

'We have no idea, but every time the translator has suggested bringing the social worker in, Aki has furiously protested.'

'Beatrice!' Julia said triumphantly.

'Beatrice from Theatres? What about her?' Tess asked.

'Beatrice speaks Japanese. Let me have a word with her and see if she can drop in now and then. Aki might benefit from some chats in his native tongue.'

Zac nodded. 'It's worth a try.' He made a note on Aki's chart. 'Also, Tess, ask the social worker to write a list of questions and the next time the translator or Beatrice is around, have them ask Aki—subtly, of course—to see if we can't determine what's really bothering him.'

'I'll see what I can organise,' Tess agreed with a smile at Zac.

'Let us know how it goes,' he replied. 'Great. Well, we might go and see Bianca Hayden next. Come along, Julia.' With that, Zac walked out of the nurses' station and over to Bianca's private room. The thirty-nine-year-old businesswoman was now one week post-op and was driving the nursing staff insane with her constant demands.

Bianca was still in traction and definitely in one of her moods.

'How are you today, Ms Hayden?' Zac asked as he crossed to the foot of her bed and took up her chart. He scanned it for a moment before passing it to Julia.

'How do you think?' Bianca answered rudely. 'I loathe being stuck in this place. At least I've been relocated into this private little…box, for want of a better word, and away from the riff-raff. I *am* a private patient, you know. Why can't you just transfer me to a private hospital? I have insurance, you know.'

'So you've mentioned.' Zac smiled. 'Unfortunately, Ms Hayden, my response is still the same as it was when you asked me yesterday. I can't risk moving you at this stage. You could do more permanent damage and your recovery time would increase.'

'I just can't accept that, Doctor,' she said primly. 'Not at all. I have a business to run and was told the other day that I have to use the hospital phone to make my calls rather than my mobile. Your nursing staff *actually* took my phone away from me yesterday. Confiscated it. It's private property, Doctor, and I want it back. I told them I'd be speaking with you at the first available opportunity. I'm a *private* patient and I'm uncomfortable enough as it is…' she gestured to her traction '…without having hospital staff taking my private possessions away, only to probably run up hundreds of dollars' worth of calls on it.'

'Ms Hayden.' Zac patiently smiled his winning smile. 'Even the *doctors* aren't allowed to use their mobile phones within the hospital grounds. The signals from them can interfere with the equipment. Heart monitors, respirators, that type of thing can be badly damaged from too much interference, which is why the hospital has the policy that no mobile phones are to be used.

'Your phone was only taken away from you because one of the nursing staff caught you using it for the third time. It just won't do. It's too dangerous.'

Julia could see him clenching his jaw but his smile was still in place, his voice calm and collected.

'But I'm in traction,' Bianca argued.

'I know but that's not an excuse.' He paused for a moment and frowned. 'I thought you were handing most of your immediate work to your assistant.'

'I fired her,' Bianca stated bluntly. 'Completely incompetent, she was.'

Zac's gaze briefly met Julia's. She read his mounting frustration and she smiled encouragingly. Bianca Hadyen had been argumentative every single day and she guessed this was half the reason Zac brought her in—to help him control his frustration.

'I see. Is there anyone else at your office that you can trust?'

'Absolutely no one, so you see the importance of why I need to get back to work? I'm a small business, Doctor, and if I cease to conduct business, I'll lose business. Probably everything.' Her tone broke on the last word and Julia watched her carefully to see whether this was just a ploy or whether she was seriously worried. After a moment, she concluded that Bianca appeared quite genuine but, then, who wouldn't be if their business was about to go down the drain?

'Bianca,' Zac said softly, and she looked at him in surprise. It was the first time he'd ever called her by her first name and it definitely had an effect. Julia tried not to smile. How did he manage to wind women around his little finger simply by saying their names? He'd been doing it for years and it never failed to amaze her. Charm. She guessed it all came down to charm.

'I completely understand what you're saying and you've stressed often enough just how important your business is to you. I'm not diminishing that in any way but the point is, you need to be relaxed and calm or your body will take longer to recover. Now the last thing you want is to be in here...' he spread his arms wide, indicating the room '...any longer than necessary which, as we've discussed, is going to be for at least the next five weeks. What we *need* to find is a way for you to continue with your business, as well as relaxing enough to recover properly.'

'What do you have in mind?' Bianca's tone was less forceful and Julia was glad Zac had managed to get through to her—on this occasion. Who knew what she'd be like the next time they came through the door?

'I need to make some calls first but hopefully we can come up with something to help you. After all, it's *you* we're most concerned about. Isn't that right, Dr Bolton?'

'Ah, absolutely,' Julia replied, trying to get her brain in gear. She'd been busy watching the way Zac had charmed the fierce businesswoman and trying to figure exactly what his secret was, rather than paying attention to what he'd been saying.

'Leave it with me and I'll get back to you—hopefully today.'

'All right, then,' Bianca agreed reluctantly.

When they'd left her room, Julia shook her head in disbelief.

'What?' he asked, grinning at her.

'You charmer, you. You had her right in the palm of your hand.'

'I know.'

'Charming *and* conceited,' she teased. 'Yep. Some things never change.'

Zac laughed, not taking her words to heart as they walked through the ward.

'So, what brilliant scheme have you got up your sleeve to help Bianca Hayden recover without the stress of having her business going down the drain?'

'Mona,' he said simply.

Julia stopped walking and looked at him. 'Of course. After all, she did used to be Jeffrey's secretary, but will she do it?'

'For me? She might. For Jeffrey?'

'Definitely,' they both said together.

'So, have you been taking your anti-inflammatories like a good little doctor?' he asked as they walked to clinic.

'And if I haven't?' she queried, her gaze quickly travelling down to his shoes and back again. He looked incredible today. Wearing a blue shirt that matched the colour of his eyes and his university tie, Julia could quite easily have spent her entire day staring at him. Instead, she had patients to see and a clinic to get through. Not to mention the mountain of paperwork that awaited her attention.

'Then I'll have to…ring your mother and conspire with her to get you to take them.'

'Ha. If you think you can wrap my mother around your little finger like you do every other female you come into contact with, then you've got another think coming, Dr Carmichael.'

He stopped at the clinic door, his arm on the handle, and she waited for him to open it. He paused, looked down into her face and wiggled his eyebrows mischievously, 'Wanna bet?'

'Zac.' She laughed and gave him a playful nudge. Oh, she so enjoyed times like these. He'd been right last week when he'd said they'd always been good friends. Being able to joke and share had been a vital part of their relationship.

They walked through the waiting room and said good morning to the staff before heading down the corridor to the consulting rooms.

'Ready to begin?' Dorothy, the clinic sister, asked, and Julia nodded, the smile still on her face. 'I see that our Dr Carmichael is already making a lasting impression on you.'

Julia laughed. 'He did that quite a few years ago.'

When Dorothy's eyebrows hit her hairline in surprise, Julia asked, 'Hasn't the grapevine been buzzing with the gossip?' When Dorothy shook her head, Julia shrugged. 'We studied at medical school together.'

'Really? How interesting? Then you'd know his sister Vanessa?'

'Yes. That's how I met Zac. Vanessa and I were good friends.'

'A bright girl, that. I used to be a theatre sister in the vascular department in Brisbane before my husband retired and decided to move us to the Gold Coast. Vanessa Ferguson is now one of the top vascular surgeons in the country. I have a lot of respect for her.'

Julia nodded. 'I couldn't agree with you more, even if she *did* pip me at the post for dux of our year.'

'No ill feelings?' Dorothy asked.

'None. Vanessa deserved it.'

'Vanessa deserved what?' Zac asked, coming up behind them.

'To be named dux for our year.'

'She's a smart little cookie, my sister. Takes after her brother,' he said, and preened with his tie.

'Ha. Look at him,' Julia said to Dorothy. 'Still as modest as the day I met him.'

Dorothy chuckled and Zac frowned at them both. 'Are

we going to start this clinic or stand about chatting all day long?'

'That's a tough one. Can we think about it?' Julia asked, but Zac simply laughed, took a set of case notes from the top of the pile and handed it to Dorothy.

'I'll be in consulting room two, Rodney's already in consulting room one and if Dr Bolton finally decides to do some work, she can see the patients in consulting room three.' With that, he turned and headed into his room.

'I haven't seen Zac this happy in a very long time,' Dorothy murmured. 'You're good for him, Julia.'

# CHAPTER SEVEN

THE comment made Julia wonder why Dorothy would say such a thing. It was obvious the clinic sister had known Zac for a while. Had there been a time when he'd been terribly unhappy? Her first patient was shown through so there was no time for further reflection, but she tucked it into the back of her mind to delve into later.

When there was a brief lull between her patients, Julia phoned Emergency Theatres to check when Beatrice was next rostered on, and couldn't believe her luck when Beatrice herself answered the phone.

They discussed Aki's situation and his slow recovery, with Beatrice promising to visit him at the end of her shift. Julia quickly called Zac in his consulting room to tell him the good news.

After clinic, Julia returned to her office to deal with some paperwork. If she could make a dent in it now, hopefully within the next few weeks she'd be up to date with the backlog of work she'd inherited and could give her complete attention to the paperwork she was generating all on her own.

At six thirty, just as Julia was starting to pack up, there was a knock on her door.

'It's open.' She looked up to find Zac standing in front of her, grinning like a Cheshire cat. 'Hi. I didn't know you were still here.' Her whole body had zinged to life the instant he'd walked into the room and now she was trying to control it. Friends, she reminded herself.

He nodded. 'I've just finished speaking to Jeffrey and then Mona.'

'So I take it by the silly grin on your face that you've been successful in your plan?'

'Naturally. Did you really expect anything else from the great Zachary Carmichael?'

Julia laughed. 'I'm not going to touch *that* one,' she said with a twinkle in her eyes. She'd finished packing her briefcase and, after collecting her bag and keys, she pointed to the door. 'Why don't you tell me about it on the way to the ward? I presume that's where you're headed next? To tell Bianca Hayden the good news?'

'I sure am.' He stepped back so she could close and lock her office door. 'Mona is magnificent,' he told her as they headed out of the department. 'She's agreed to come in tomorrow morning after ward round to meet Bianca and we'll take it from there. Right now, I want to impress on Bianca how generous this is of Mona so hopefully Bianca will behave with respect and gratitude towards her when she comes in tomorrow.'

Julia agreed. 'I think part of her problem with firing staff and being awful to the nurses is that she's simply frustrated. I would be, too, if my business looked as though it would go down the drain because I was laid up in hospital through no fault of my own.'

'Also, when I was talking to Mona, she asked about Aki Ishimaru. I told her the status and she said after she'd finished with Bianca, she'd stop by and talk to him as well, agreeing that the more people he spoke to in his native language, the quicker his recovery should be. Unfortunately, he's still not well enough to be transferred back to Japan. His asthma could flare up at any time and his progress, as you know, has been very slow.'

'I have this calming sensation that once Mona becomes involved with both of these patients, they'll pick right up.'

'You're probably right. You've known her longer than I have.' They both spoke to Bianca, who was delighted at the prospect of someone—a stranger—willing to help her out. She also expressed her extreme gratitude to Zac for helping her. Julia was again bemused at the effect he had on women! She supposed it was because he *was* a nice, caring man. It was that simple.

After obtaining a promise from Bianca that she would be nice and co-operative when Mona arrived in the morning, Julia let Zac go and see Lucas by himself. She didn't want another argument or to exacerbate Lucas's condition. When Zac returned, he told her that Lucas had responded well to the second course of antibiotics and was being discharged.

'Good. Let's see how Aki is doing.'

He was quiet and unresponsive. Julia's concerns increased. There had to be something else wrong for him to be listless like this. They checked his chart which showed a very slight improvement which was better than nothing. They read the nursing report which stated that Aki had been more settled this evening than previously and that the extra visits from both the translator and Beatrice, might be the contributing factors.

Zac walked Julia out to her car, saying that it was hospital policy that all female staff be walked to their cars either by Security or a trusted male colleague after dark.

'Another one of Jeffrey's rules,' he added. 'And I can't say I blame him.'

'It's second nature to me,' she told him as she put her bag and briefcase into her car. 'The same rule applied at the hospital in Perth.'

He nodded and held the driver's door open for her while

she climbed in. He closed the door and waited for her to wind down the window. Leaning down, he smiled at her, their faces now quite close together.

'Goodnight, Julia.' His tone was husky, his gaze filled with desire. Julia swallowed, knowing her gaze reciprocated his feelings.

'Night,' she replied, and cleared her throat. Oh, kiss me, Zac. Just go ahead and do it, her mind silently screamed. Neither of them moved.

'Drive safely,' he whispered.

'See you tomorrow.'

Still, neither of them moved. Her heart was pounding so wildly against her ribs she was certain he could hear it. Her lips parted as her breathing increased, her gaze flicking between his mesmerising blue eyes and his parted lips.

'Bye.' As though exerting superhuman effort, Zac stood and patted the roof of her car.

Julia closed her eyes for a brief second, trying to gather her wits. How was she supposed to drive a car after an intensely sensual and frustrating moment like that? She forced her sluggish brain to kick in as she reached out her hand and started the engine.

She smiled and waved as Zac stood in the parking lot, watching her leave. 'Friendship,' she mumbled as she drove carefully out of the hospital grounds and onto the road.

She didn't sleep well that night and it had nothing to do with her bruised coccyx!

On Tuesday, her back was feeling even better. She had an awful bruise on her arm and back and a few on her legs, which she was discovering as they appeared. The anti-inflammatories were working well and she was sure she'd be able to handle the drive to Brisbane on the weekend to see Vanessa.

Mona was on the ward at the appointed time and both Zac and Julia welcomed her warmly. They took her through to see Bianca Hayden and introduced them. After a few minutes they left them alone, noting that Bianca *did* seem to be on her best behaviour.

'I've asked Mona to page either one of us when she's finished,' Zac told her. 'I'd like us to be there when she goes to see Aki Ishimaru.'

Julia nodded. 'Good thinking.' She sorted through some more paperwork and ate lunch before receiving a page. She glanced at the number—the ward. Mona must be ready so she locked her office before heading there.

When she arrived, Zac and Mona were talking quietly in the nurses' station obviously waiting for her.

'How did it go with Bianca?' she asked, and Zac smiled.

'Bianca is now the happiest I've ever seen her and is actually looking relaxed.'

'Marvellous Mona strikes again,' Julia said with a smile, and Mona laughed.

'You're both flattering me and you know you shouldn't.' She hesitated for a moment before acquiescing. 'But if you insist upon it, don't let me stop you.'

They all laughed. 'I presume Zac's briefed you on Aki's situation?' Julia asked.

'Yes.' Mona sobered. 'What I'd like you to do, Julia, is to take me over there and after a minute or two have your pager go off so it doesn't look quite like a set-up. Zac, you stay here and page her.'

'Why can't I go over, too?' he asked.

'My hunch,' Mona said softly and both Zac and Julia leaned forward a little so they could hear her, 'is that Aki thinks he's lost face.'

Julia frowned. 'It wasn't his fault he was injured.'

'Still,' Mona continued, 'if a man is there, it would

make him feel all the more awkward. Then again, he probably doesn't want to be surrounded by females either.' She shook her head. 'We're just going to have to do the best we can. Pull the curtains around us as well, to ensure a bit of privacy for him. I know the other patients might not be able to understand what we're talking about but hopefully it will help Aki to relax a little while we talk.'

Zac bent down and kissed Mona's cheek. 'You've missed your calling in life,' he told her.

'On the contrary,' Julia said. 'How do you think Jeffrey's risen to his current position as director without the help and support of his beautiful wife?'

'I'm beginning to think that it's not Jeffrey who's always right, but Mona.'

The woman in question smiled at them both before inclining her head in Aki's direction. 'Let's go, Julia.'

Everything went according to plan. Julia pulled the curtain around them and left Mona to do the introductions in Japanese. She translated Aki's replies for Julia, which stated that he was happy with his treatment and very grateful. Soon Julia's pager sounded and she excused herself, returning to the nurses' station to wait with Zac.

After ten minutes, with no sign of Mona coming out, Julia consulted the clock on the wall. 'I've waited as long as I can,' she told him. 'I'm going to be late for my elective operating list if I don't leave now.'

'Go. I'll call through to Theatre if there's any dramatic breakthrough.'

'There won't be,' Julia prophesied. 'Mona would never push him that far, that soon. She'll establish a rapport with Aki before anything concrete comes out but, on the bright side, it's one more person for Aki to be conversing with in his own language.'

'True.'

'Just make sure you catch up with me after Theatre and let me know what happens.'

'Will do,' he said. 'Have fun in Theatre.'

'Gee, thanks.' She smiled at him before leaving the ward.

Her operating session went off without complications. Her one and only patient was the man who'd been admitted in the early hours of the previous Saturday morning and required knee reconstruction. It was a long and drawn-out process, which required her constant concentration and drained her energy. Her back felt stiff and sore afterwards but there was nothing much she could do except rest it.

Returning to her office, she forced herself to look on the optimistic side. Her patient would make a complete recovery and she was very much looking forward to the debrief Zac was supposed to give her on Aki's meeting with Mona.

'Things went well,' he told her after finding her in her office. 'You were right about Mona wanting to build up a level of trust. I've just been down to review him and he's more settled than he's been in a long time.'

'She's a miracle-worker,' Julia agreed.

'I'll say and what's more, Bianca Hayden is being nice to the nursing staff.'

Julia laughed. 'Wonders will never cease.' She winced as she shifted in her chair and Zac's mirth faded.

'How's your back?'

'Sore,' she admitted, and shrugged. 'It's just from operating this afternoon. I'll head home now, have something to eat and take the anti-inflammatories.' She started to tidy up.

'Good idea. I'll walk you to your car,' he stated.

Julia stopped and glared at him. He had to be joking! She didn't think she could handle a repeat of last night's performance when he'd come *so* close to kissing her, only to leave her high and dry. She had been addicted to him years ago and now seemed to be no different. She was hooked on his kisses, his arms around her and the smouldering look of desire in his eyes.

'Don't worry about it, Zac. I'll get one of the security guards to walk me.'

He looked at her for a long moment, a flash of desire visible in the blue depths of his eyes before it was quickly veiled. Her heart picked up the familiar irregular rhythm it developed whenever he looked at her like that.

'Right. Good idea,' he agreed as though he, too, was having a difficult time controlling himself.

On Saturday morning, Julia was outside, packing her car, ready for the trip to Brisbane. Cassandra had opted to stay at home, thereby having a relaxing weekend all to herself.

'See how some bad things can turn out to be for the best?'

'What do you mean, Mum?' Julia asked as she carried another suitcase out to her car.

'Well if you hadn't bruised your coccyx, then Zac probably wouldn't have offered to drive you to Brisbane this weekend. He would have just given you the address and met you there.'

'Hmm,' Julia replied, and headed back inside. 'Edward,' she called. 'Honey, it's time to go.' She picked up another bag. 'Even though I feel fine, it *is* nice that we're all going together and it's just as well we're taking *my* car,' she added. 'There's no way we'd have squished all of this stuff into Zac's Jaguar.'

As she headed outside again, Zac pulled up. Julia looked over her shoulder at her mother. 'Take Edward to the toilet, please? I don't want to keep Zac waiting.'

'Righty-ho,' Cassandra answered, and Julia continued on her way.

Zac walked up the driveway with a small overnight bag in his hand. 'Did I say we were going for a week? I meant to say week*end*. How much stuff have you got in there?' he asked, peering into the boot of her car.

Julia hoisted the last bag in and looked at Zac. 'When you travel with children, it doesn't matter whether you're going for one night or one month—you still pack the same amount of stuff. Put your bag in and I'll get this closed.'

He did as she suggested and she closed the boot. 'Now, I just need some things for him to play with in the car as we're travelling and we're set.'

'Is all of that stuff *really* for Edward?' he asked sceptically.

'No.' Julia shook her head and smiled, heading back inside. 'Edward?' she called again from the door as she picked up a bag of cars and trains for him to play with for the hour-long drive to Vanessa's house.

'Tumming, Mummy,' he called, and she could hear him running through the house towards her. 'I'm so *escited*,' he said, jumping up and down to prove it.

'Me, too,' she told him, and scooped him up. 'Give Grandma a kiss goodbye.'

'Bye, Gr'ma,' he said, and wrapped his arms around her mother's neck. When he'd finished, Julia followed suit.

'Have a nice relaxing and peaceful time,' she told her mother.

'You, too, if that's at all possible with the dashing Dr Carmichael right beside you,' her mother whispered. They all walked out to the car.

Zac greeted Cassandra and handed over the keys to his Jag. 'What? Really?' the older woman said in astonishment. 'You're trusting me to drive it?'

'If you trust yourself,' he said with a smile. 'After all, you've effectively been left without a car.'

'I *had* planned on doing a lot of walking this weekend.'

'Now you don't have to,' he replied. Julia buckled Edward into his seat, listening to the exchange between the other two adults.

'Well, thank you, Zac. I'll park it in the garage directly you're gone and shall take very good care of it.'

'I'm sure you will.' He gave her a nod and walked around to the driver's seat. Soon they were off, driving through the already busy streets towards the motorway. They listened to some music and talked over old times while Edward played quietly in the back with his toys.

'He's very good,' Zac commented as he indicated to exit the motorway.

'Thank you,' Julia responded proudly. 'He always has been.'

'Was it difficult? I mean, giving birth to him without having your husband there for support?' he asked quietly, glancing in the rear-view mirror to ensure Edward hadn't heard.

Julia shrugged. 'Mum was there. Mona and Jeffrey were pacing up and down in the waiting room. They're all the family we need.' Julia glanced back at her son who was completely engrossed with what he was doing. She sighed. 'I think I've mentioned before that Ian has absolutely no interest in Edward whatsoever, and he doesn't pay maintenance.'

'That's a bit harsh, isn't it?'

'Are you criti—?'

'Steady on, Jules. I'm not having a go at you, I'm having a go at *him*. How dare he leave you in the lurch like that? Treat you the way he did. It's not what marriage is about.'

Julia laughed ironically. 'Oh, and I'd suppose you'd know? You've shied away from marriage all of your life, Zac, but at least you're open and honest about it.'

He was silent for a while and she heard him grinding his teeth. 'You're angry. What have I said?' she asked quietly.

'It's nothing,' he said, and turned a corner.

'No. It's not nothing, Zac. What's wrong?'

He slowed the car before pulling into a driveway and cutting the engine. Julia looked briefly up at the large house in front of them before returning her attention to the man sitting beside her. 'Zac?' she pleaded as he ran a hand through his hair. Angry *and* frustrated. Something was definitely wrong.

The car was silent except for the truck noises that Edward was making in the back, totally engrossed in his own little world. With every passing second Julia could feel Zac withdrawing from her, and her anxiety began to increase.

'I know about marriage, Julia.' His tone was emotionless, his features now bland. 'Because I've *been* married.'

# CHAPTER EIGHT

JULIA felt her jaw drop open but there was no way she could have stopped it. She also knew her expression radiated complete amazement and shock. 'You...you were *married*? The man who swore he'd *never* enter the state of matrimony?'

Zac's answer was to pull the keys from the ignition and open the door. Julia reached out for his arm but he was too quick for her.

'We here, Mum? We here?' Edward asked from the back.

'Yes, darling. We're here. Undo your seat belt and pack up your toys,' she instructed as she watched Zac walk up the path towards his sister's front door. She clenched her jaw and shook her head. All this time they'd spent together during the past weeks and he hadn't thought to volunteer the information at all.

Julia took her seat belt off and climbed out of the car, resisting the urge to slam the door shut. Instead, she waited patiently for her son whilst seething inside with building anger towards Zac.

Ever since she'd arrived back in town two weeks ago, he'd made her feel guilty for having a son. For wanting a commitment. Ten years ago, they'd parted ways because Zac hadn't wanted to get married or have a family and *now* he was telling her that he'd been married! That was rich!

The confession had brought with it several questions that Julia wanted answers to. The top of the list was *who*?

*Who* had been the woman he'd married? Where was she now? How long had they been divorced?

Another thought dawned. So *that's* what he'd meant last week when he'd said he wouldn't go through it *again*. Pennies were starting to drop, but she still felt very hurt and betrayed that he hadn't said anything sooner.

Her entire level of trust in Zac was now questionable. She took a deep breath and escorted Edward up the path towards the door where Zac was standing, pressing the doorbell again.

'They're probably out the back in the pool,' he said, not meeting her gaze. 'The twins, Bobby and Wendy, love an early morning swim.'

'And they're almost seven?' she asked, making sure she had everyone straight. She was starting to get nervous knots in her stomach as they continued to stand at the front door.

'That's right, and Travis is three, like Edward.' Zac glanced down at Julia's son, only to find the little boy looking right back up at him. Edward smiled and Zac's gut twisted. He *was* cute, no doubt about that. He might not have his mother's dark brown eyes but he certainly had a lot of her expressions. He was a good kid, too, and Zac wondered why he'd been surprised. He should have known that Julia would have everything in hand—she always had. Super-efficient, super-organised and super-sexy.

He looked away, trying to control his thoughts. 'This is ridiculous,' he said as he headed around the side of the house. 'Come on,' he urged impatiently when Julia didn't move.

Zac stuck his hand over the fence and opened the gate that led to the back of the property. He waited for Julia and Edward to come through before walking up the path.

'Hello?' he bellowed loudly as they rounded the corner to the back.

'Zac?' His sister, wearing a bright red bathing-suit, was sitting on a step in the shallow end of the pool, her blonde hair pinned up on top of her head, out of the way. Her husband was holding onto Travis who had armbands on, while the twins splashed in the deeper water.

Zac smiled and waved as the twins started squealing, 'Uncle Zac! Uncle Zac's here.'

'Julia!' Vanessa squealed, and was out of the pool in one swift motion, gathering her towel around her wet body and rushing towards them. Julia held tightly to Edward's hand as he loved swimming pools and was usually quite impatient to get in the water. She held out her free arm towards Vanessa and the two friends embraced, tears of joy in their eyes.

'Wow! I can't believe it's really you,' Vanessa said softly as they broke apart and looked at each other. 'I have missed you *so* much.'

'I know what you mean,' Julia replied, smiling as she brushed a tear from her cheek. She sniffed and they both laughed. Edward was tugging on her hand.

'I go swimming, Mummy. Swimming.'

'Yes, all right, Edward. Just a minute. Come and say hello to one of Mummy's special friends.'

Vanessa crouched down so she was at Edward's eye level. 'Hello, handsome,' she said. 'What have you got there?' She pointed to his favourite toy which was tucked firmly under his arm.

Edward showed her his favourite character from a popular television show and smiled brightly at the new friend he'd found.

Zac watched the exchange with a tightening of his chest. He looked at Julia and found her smiling proudly down at her son. Good. She should be proud. He glanced over at Vanessa's family in the pool, all laughing and having fun. A *family*. It brought back too many memories of Cara, too many hurts, and there was no way Zac was going to allow himself to be hurt again.

Clenching his jaw, he turned to his sister.

'I'll head on inside and then start unpacking the car.'

'Want a hand?' Mike, his brother-in-law, called from the pool.

'No, thanks.' Zac forced a smile and waved. He looked at Julia. 'You two girls catch up.'

'Uncle Zac,' Wendy called. 'Come in the pool.'

'Soon,' he answered, and hurried inside. After he'd unloaded the stuff, Zac started to feel in better control. Too many kids, too many happy families, bringing back too many memories.

Cara and the memories from his marriage usually surfaced whenever he came around to Vanessa's house, and they all knew it. Even though it had been over three years since her death, Zac was still running from the hurt.

'Everything all right?' Vanessa said from behind him, and he turned, a pasted-on smile on his lips.

'Fine.' He placed his arm about her shoulder when she gave him a hug. 'How about you? Recovered from your trip overseas?'

'Yes,' she said with relief. 'Back home and relaxing. I've got another week off before I head back to work.'

'So where is it?' he asked.

'It's over here,' Vanessa said, and rushed to the display cabinet in the lounge room. Zac followed her and she handed him the wall plaque with her name engraved on a shiny new nameplate.

'Wow. My little sister winning the award for most outstanding medical breakthrough in vascular surgery,' he said, and kissed her. 'I'm so proud of you.'

'Thanks. Now, tell me, what's going on between you and Julia?'

Zac's earlier frown returned. 'Nothing. We're friends.'

'Oh, don't give me that. The tension in the air is exactly what it used to be when you dated years ago. Are you going to stand there and seriously tell me that you feel nothing but *friendship* for Julia?'

'No,' he said after a pause. 'I'm not going to tell you anything because it's none of your business, little sister,' he said in a forced jovial tone. Now was not the time to have a deep and meaningful discussion about Julia.

'What do you *mean*, none of my business? I was the one who first introduced you. You're my brother—she's one of my closest friends. The fact that you're refusing to answer any questions *means* there's more going on here than you want me to know.'

'So why don't you take the hint and stop asking questions, then?' he asked with an infuriating smile. 'When you probe, Vanessa, you don't know when to quit, and you keep on probing.'

'Hey, I'm a surgeon. I like to know what's going on, deep down inside.'

'Well, I'm not your patient, sis.'

'But, Zac, she's here—you're here—'

'Shh.' Zac placed a hand over her mouth. 'Not another word, Vanessa. I'm just not in the mood.'

'Sorry to interrupt,' Julia said from the doorway, Edward's hand still held firmly in hers. Both of them turned to look at her, guilty looks on their faces, and she assumed they'd been discussing her. She pointed to her bags which Zac had left in the hallway. 'Edward's getting impatient to get into the pool so I thought I'd get our swimmers out now.'

'Sure,' Vanessa said. 'I'll show you where you'll be sleeping tonight. Is this one yours?'

'No. That *one* is mine.' Zac collected his bag, picking up one of Julia's in his other hand. 'The other five bags belong to Julia.'

'And her son,' Vanessa defended, and turned to Julia. 'You don't need to tell me about travelling with children. Taking the three of them overseas was hectic—but a lot of fun. It was well worth the effort.' She headed up the stairs and they all followed.

'I go swimming, Mummy,' Edward was demanding.

'Yes, darling, but you need to get changed first. You don't want to get your clothes all wet, do you?'

'No.'

'All right, then.'

'Edward,' Vanessa said, 'can you guess what colour your room might be?'

'Um, bwue?'

'No, it's not blue.'

'Um, wed?'

'Not red.'

'Um, gween?'

'Yes,' Vanessa exclaimed with delight as she opened a door for them and walked into the room. 'Look it's green. You were right.'

'I was wight, Mummy. I was wight,' Edward chanted, as he jumped up and down excitedly.

'Look at this lovely green room,' Julia said, and pointed to the pastel green walls.

'I love gween. I love gween. I's my fabourite.'

'Zac, you're next door,' Vanessa said. 'The bathroom is

opposite these rooms and you're the only three who'll be using it so make yourselves at home.'

'Thank you.' Julia's thanks were heartfelt and she reached out to hug her friend again. 'Thank you so much for having us.'

'My pleasure,' Vanessa replied.

'I go swimming, *peeze*, *Mummy*!' Edward demanded, and both women laughed.

'I see he has the usual three-year-old patience,' Vanessa said. 'We'll leave you to get changed. Come on, Zac,' she said as she walked out. 'Can you guess what colour *your* room might be?'

Julia shut the door, giggling like a schoolgirl. Oh, this was great. Fantastic! Right at this moment, she didn't want to think about Zac or the fact that he'd been married. She wanted to concentrate on her son and relaxing and having a good time. The thinking would come later—it always did.

Soon they had changed into their swimsuits and were walking down the stairs. Julia had made sure that Edward had a special swimming T-shirt on as well and had applied sunscreen to the parts of his body that weren't covered up. Armbands had been inflated, so that Edward could quite easily float in the water by himself.

She wore a black one-piece swimsuit, nothing fancy, just sensibly cut. Slathering her body with sunscreen, as she hated to burn, Julia and Edward made their way out to the pool.

Zac was already in the water, playing with the twins. Their gazes met and held before his quickly appraised her slender body. She felt herself begin to blush, so lowered her head to look at her son. They'd brought their own towels and she placed them on one of the chairs as Edward was tugging furiously on her arm.

'*Tum on, Mummy,*' he urged.

'All right.' Julia stepped onto the first step and squealed.

The twins laughed and Zac smiled. 'It gets easier with each step you take,' he said. 'And a swim is just what your doctor is ordering to ease the stiffness in your back.'

Julia pulled a face at him. 'Know-all,' she accused lightly, and he laughed. The deep, rich, sound washed over her and she shivered, rubbing her arms.

'It's not *that* bad,' Mike said as he gently swung Travis around. 'Just dive right in. Get it over and done with quickly.'

'Once you're in, it's not so cool,' Vanessa offered from behind them as she, too, came back into the pool.

It was a beautiful sunny day with the temperature quite high. A nice cool dip was what they all needed but Julia wished the water was just a few degrees warmer! She decided to take Mike's advice and asked Vanessa to hold Edward's hand for a moment.

'Big breath,' Zac teased, just before Julia dived beneath the water.

'Ooh,' she gasped as she came up seconds later, and they all laughed. 'When? When does it get better?' she demanded. She held her arms out to Edward who was squealing with delight. He let go of Vanessa's hand and jumped towards his mother, sending a spray of water all over her. 'Just as well I was already wet,' she said with a laugh.

They all played for about an hour, sometimes making up games and sometimes just moving about. Julia was relaxing and having fun. Zac seemed to be doing the same, and for the moment the unspoken truce they'd called was lovely.

Mike cooked a barbeque for lunch and they all ate their fill. Afterwards, the twins started climbing a tree in the backyard and Travis and Edward were happily playing with their cars. Mike and Vanessa had gone inside to take care of the dirty dishes, insisting that their guests stay outside and relax.

Zac sat down in the deckchair next to Julia, who was by the pool. 'Having a good time?'

She turned and smiled at him. 'Oh, yes. It's great. I'd forgotten what good fun Vanessa could be.'

'Hey? What about me? Weren't we the Three Musketeers?'

'Hmm...' She pretended to consider the question thoughtfully for a moment before smiling. 'Were you good fun? Let's not go there right now, Zac,' she said with a laugh.

'How's your back feeling?'

'Much better.' He made her report in every morning on the status of her bruised coccyx.

'Good, but, still, take it easy. Did you take your anti-inflammatories this morning?'

'Yes, Doctor,' she jested, and he laughed.

They started talking about a controversial article they'd both read in a medical journal about pelvic fractures, discussing the pros and cons of a particular surgical technique. Edward came over and sat beside her for a while, yawning once or twice before going to the edge of the pool. He still had his armbands on but Julia watched him like a hawk.

'Be careful,' she warned him. He sat on the bottom step and dangled his feet in the water. They continued to talk.

'By performing an anterior and proximal incision in one go, it means there's more muscle and tendon in the way and an increased risk of cutting something we shouldn't,' Julia added.

Edward stood up and started walking around the perimeter of the pool. Again her gaze followed him, watching his every step, looking for wet spots, but the sun had dried out most of the water around the edge. 'Edward. Come here,' she said.

'No,' he answered back.

She looked at Zac. 'He's getting tired. It's been a big day for him.'

He continued to walk around the perimeter twice more. 'All right. That's enough,' she said, and when he came close, she reached out to grab him. Edward managed to elude her.

'One,' she counted as he rounded the deep end. 'Two.'

He looked up at her with a cheeky grin on his face.

'Watch what you're doing,' Julia chastised. The moment the words were out of her mouth, Edward slipped and fell. *Splash!*

'*Edward!*'

Julia was on her feet and heading for the pool, but Zac beat her to it. He dived into the water as Edward's head and shoulders bobbed up, his armbands keeping him up, but as his hands were splashing about as he started to panic, his head went under again.

Zac lifted him up and held him firmly in his arms as he waded back through the pool towards the steps. Edward clung to him, his arms wrapped tightly around Zac's neck. Julia had a towel ready as Zac handed him over.

'He's fine. Just a little shaken up.'

Mike and Vanessa had come out of the house at Julia's cry, and the other three children were all crowding around Edward.

'He's fine,' Zac said reassuringly. Julia sat down with Edward who was crying with both shock and tiredness.

'You're all right,' she told him. 'You're a gooseygander some days.' She cradled him tightly and kissed his head. 'How about you and Mummy go for another swim in a few minutes?'

'Me, too,' said Travis.

'Us, too,' the twins piped up.

'Sounds like another pool party,' Vanessa agreed. 'You just need to wait for...' she consulted the clock inside '...another twenty minutes to let your lunch settle properly.'

When the crowd had disbursed and Edward had snuggled into his mother for a little cat-nap, Julia looked across at Zac. 'Thank you,' she said, her eyes filling with tears and spilling over her lashes onto her cheeks.

'Hey,' he said softly, and reached over to tenderly wipe the tears away. 'It's all part of the service. He'll be fine,' he reiterated.

'Oh, I know, but it's that millisecond heart-stopping moment of dread that takes a while to get over.'

He nodded. 'You'll be fine.' Zac smiled at her and Julia knew in that instant that she was head over heels in love with him. *When* it had happened she wasn't quite sure. Whether she'd never really *stopped* loving him was quite on the cards, but of one thing she was now positively sure. She was in love with Zachary Carmichael and there was nothing she could do about it.

Zac looked at Edward who had his eyes closed, relaxing in the secure comfort of his mother's embrace. It wasn't right that such a cute little fellow should grow up without a father. Zac's dislike for Julia's ex-husband grew. During the time he'd spent with Edward today, Zac had come to realise that he *liked* the boy. Liked him for himself, not just because he was Julia's son.

There was no doubting the attraction between himself and Julia and, regardless of how many times they fought it, it still managed to overwhelm them. One thing was for sure—Zac knew he had to tell her about his past. If there was ever going to be anything more between them, then the past had to be laid to rest. The question he had to ask himself was, was he capable of doing it?

Later that night, after the children were all settled in bed, Julia went downstairs to join the adults. They all talked for a while about various topics and Mike urged the three of them to recount some of their medical school anecdotes.

Just before midnight, Vanessa and Mike said goodnight and headed upstairs.

'I'd better get some sleep as well,' Julia said, smothering a yawn. 'The time went so quickly, I had no idea it was so late.'

'You don't have to go—on account of me, that is,' Zac said softly as he came to sit beside her on the sofa.

Julia smiled. 'No, it's not because of you. It's because my son wakes up at six-thirty on the dot every morning and demands his mother's attention!' Despite what had transpired between them either in the past or in the last few weeks, Julia *loved* being in his company. She knew there was still a lot to be said between them but for now she was quite content to let the unspoken words remain unspoken.

'Have you had a relaxing day?' he asked, his arm leaning across the back of the sofa, his body angled towards her.

'Yes, except for when Edward fell into the pool.' Julia shuddered as the terrifying memory flooded back. 'I knew he'd be all right. He had his armbands on and it was only a few seconds before you plucked him from the water...' She smiled gratefully at him. 'But, still, I feel awful. I should have stood up and gone and got him. He wasn't listening to me, wasn't obeying verbal commands, which he's usually *very* good at. He was tired and impatient and that's usually the sign that I go and get him to ensure he doesn't hurt himself.'

Zac shook his head. 'Don't beat yourself up about it, Julia. You were watching him, you'd protected him as best you could and if he hadn't panicked, he would have been as right as rain. When you took him in the pool later on, he was quite happy about it. I'll bet you, right now the thought has completely gone from his head with no horrible after-effects.'

She shuddered again. 'No. Just after-effects for his mother.'

Zac moved closer. 'You're a terrific mother, Jules. You love him with every fibre of your being and he loves you back. The emotion isn't forced—it's given freely, from *both* sides. He's a credit to you.' Zac's tone was quiet and sincere.

Julia's smile had become wobbly and her eyes started to mist with tears. 'Thank you,' she said softly. 'It means a lot to hear you say that.' Especially as she knew his opinions on marriage and families. Then again, did she?

She looked down at her hands and fidgeted for a moment before looking back at him. Biting her lip, she wondered whether she had the courage to ask him about his wife. Deciding it was probably going to be now or never, she took the chance.

'Will you tell me what happened between you and your wife? Why you divorced?'

He slowly shifted in his seat, as though her words had made him uncomfortable. She had no doubt that they had. 'Don't you think you owe me at least *that* much? I've shared with you—'

He cut her off by holding up his hand for silence. She

tried to read the look in his eyes but once more found his features masked.

'I want to tell you about her, Julia, but right now...' He shook his head, unable to complete the sentence. 'It's not the right time.'

Julia's concern for him grew, along with her annoyance for his ex-wife. Why had they divorced if he still loved her so much? Obviously it had been his wife who'd wanted to end their marriage and Julia thought she must have been crazy. Who would want to end their marriage to a man like Zac? Apart from being *the* most handsome man she'd ever met, he was kind, caring and loving. What woman in her right mind would end all that willingly?

'I think I'll head up to bed,' he said, but made no move.

Julia's heart went out to him and she yearned to take him in her arms and kiss his hurt better—just like she did with Edward. Their gazes held and Julia edged a little closer. It had been a week since Zac had last kissed her and that fact alone had made the week feel as though it had dragged on for ever.

'Zac?' she whispered, and reached for his hand. He let her take it and entwined his fingers with hers. Her heart was pounding wildly against her ribs, her body was trembling slightly from an overpowering sense of love. She was glad to be sitting down because she was certain at that moment that her knees would have failed to support her.

Zac leaned forward and kissed her hand lightly before letting it go. 'Goodnight, Julia,' he whispered, and stood. She watched him go and not once did he look back. When he'd disappeared up the stairs, she stared out into the still room, her thoughts all jumbling over each other, while her brain tried to make sense of them.

\* \* \*

The following morning, Julia was awoken by her disorientated alarm clock, who climbed into bed with her at six-thirty and actually snuggled down for a good ten minutes. She thought this was bliss and realised it was probably a record for him, but soon he was asking for a pillow fight.

There was a knock on her door and she made sure the covers were pulled high around her chest before she called, 'Come in.'

Vanessa opened the door and stood in the doorway. 'Good morning. Did you both sleep well?'

'Yes.' Julia smiled and yawned.

'Edward?' Vanessa's voice and expression were filled with the promise of something good. 'Travis has just gone downstairs to watch your favourite show on television.' She pointed to the soft toy that was still in Edward's bed, the one he'd been holding yesterday when he'd met her.

'I go, too,' he said, his entire body buzzing with excitement.

'Give Mummy a kiss,' Julia instructed, and Edward quickly obliged before scrambling off her bed. He ran to his own and grabbed his soft toy before running to the door.

'Oh, the stairs,' Julia mumbled, and started to get out of bed.

'Don't worry. Bobby's coming,' Vanessa said, looking off down the hallway. 'Help Edward down the stairs, please, Bobby,' she told her oldest son.

'Uh, sure,' he replied, and when Vanessa had watched them go down, she came into Julia's room and shut the door behind her.

'So...what time did you and Zac finish talking last night?' She sat cross-legged at the end of Julia's bed.

Julia smiled. It felt just like old times. 'Not long after the two of you went to bed.'

Vanessa frowned. 'Oh.'

'Why? Were you and Mike trying to leave us alone?'

Vanessa nodded.

'Well, you shouldn't have bothered.' Julia busied herself with straightening the covers.

'What happened?'

'I asked him to tell me about his ex-wife. He said he couldn't and then he went to bed.' She shrugged dejectedly. 'I guess he needs more time.'

'When did you find out about her?'

'Yesterday. When we pulled into your driveway. He blurted out the fact that he'd been married and then walked off.'

Vanessa eyed her critically for a second before taking a deep breath.

'Oh, for heaven's sake, say it,' Julia prompted, knowing there was a burning question on Vanessa's mind.

'What are...? I mean...' She cleared her throat and tried again. 'How do you feel about Zac?'

Julia shrugged and looked at her friend. 'I feel the same way I did yesterday, only more frustrated. I know it's not easy for Zac to open up and talk about his feelings.'

'It's not easy for *any* man,' Vanessa joked and then sobered as she looked closely at her friend. 'You're still in love with him.' It was a statement, and Julia nodded.

'Yes, but I think we need time to sort a few things out, as well as getting to know each other for who we are *now*, before we can build on the attraction which hasn't diminished one iota over the past decade. After all, we've only been back in each other's lives for two weeks, which isn't long.'

'Sometimes it's long enough,' Vanessa told her. 'I knew the first time I met Mike that he was someone different, someone I could talk to. Within a week I was hopelessly in love with him, and after ten days he'd proposed and I'd accepted. We've been together ever since.'

Julia smiled. 'It sounds so nice.'

'It is. I know Zac has a lot of issues to work through, Julia, but you're his soul-mate. I feel it deep down within my bones. Just be careful,' Vanessa warned as she stood up. 'I know Zac will tell you, sooner or later, about Cara, and when he does, he may try to push you away.'

'Wouldn't it bring us closer together?'

'Not necessarily. Zac hasn't dated in over three years. Very few people at GCH know about his past, and although there may have been a bit of gossip buzzing around from people who've either worked in Sydney or heard the story at second or third hand, it's mostly old news now. Still, he keeps his professional distance from most of his colleagues, except for Jeffrey McArthur.'

'It's hard to keep your distance from Jeffrey,' Julia said with a smile. 'I have a lot of time for him. He and Mona are very special to me.'

'He *is* lovely and I'm glad he pushed Zac into going on that blind date.' Vanessa chuckled. 'Who would have thought it would have been *you*? I almost choked when Zac told me the story.' Vanessa laughed and shrugged. 'Accept it, my friend. It's fate.'

Julia showered and dressed in denim jeans and a white top, leaving her hair loose, before heading downstairs. The children were all watching television and she was pleased to see Edward having fun. She walked into the kitchen but stopped when she realised Vanessa and Zac were in the midst of another discussion. Another discussion which she was certain was about her. Zac looked great, dressed in black jeans and a white polo shirt. She licked her lips and looked away, trying to control the urge to walk across to him and claim his lips in a proper good morning kiss.

'Cool it,' she whispered, and as she wasn't sure whether to walk away or announce herself, she was glad when the decision was taken out of her hands when Vanessa looked up and saw her standing there.

'Hi, Julia. We were just talking about you,' she confessed, and Julia watched the accusing look Zac sent his sister.

'I see.' Julia walked over to the bench, unable to meet Zac's gaze directly.

'Coffee? Toast?' Vanessa asked, and Julia nodded. As Vanessa flitted around the kitchen, Zac came and sat next to Julia at the breakfast bar, a cup of coffee between his hands.

'Sleep well?' he asked, and for the first time that day she met his gorgeous blue eyes and was hard-pressed not to sigh with longing. She nodded, answering his question, but was too caught up in how gorgeous he looked to formulate a verbal reply. He was so handsome, so caring, so perfect for her that she just wanted to take his face between her hands and kiss him senseless. Couldn't he *see* that she was in love with him?

He cleared his throat and forced a smile, and she realised that he had indeed seen the spark of passion in her gaze. He shifted a little uncomfortably and Julia looked away, grateful when Vanessa placed a hot cup of coffee in front of her.

'Toast shouldn't be a minute,' she told Julia.

The room was plunged into silence, except for the faint sounds of the television coming from the other room.

'Zac just asked me to keep an eye on Edward,' Vanessa said, obviously unable to bear the silence any longer. 'He wants to show you something.'

Julia turned her head sharply and looked at him. 'What?' she asked, her voice husky and soft. She cleared her throat.

'What?' The question sounded more firm, more in control this time.

'You'll see,' he said.

'Here's your toast,' Vanessa said, and arranged an array of spreads in front of Julia. 'Help yourself. Edward's already had some cereal with Travis so don't worry about him.'

'Thank you,' Julia said warmly.

'Eat up,' Zac said. 'I'll get your car keys and then we'll go.' With that he walked out of the room.

Julia looked worriedly at Vanessa. 'What's going on?' she asked.

'Eat up and go with the man before he changes his mind,' Vanessa urged.

Julia buttered one slice of toast and added some jam. She ate and chewed so fast, she knew indigestion would probably be the result. Adding more milk to her coffee so it cooled faster, she drank most of it down before Vanessa said, 'Leave the rest and *go*!'

Julia smiled at her friend as she grabbed the piece of toast and stood up. 'Thanks for keeping an eye on Edward. I appreciate it.'

Vanessa simply shrugged. 'One more doesn't make much difference. Get going,' she urged, and Julia did as she suggested. She quickly explained to Edward that she was going out with Zac and gave him a goodbye kiss. She was pleased to see he wasn't worried as he and Travis played cars together.

She found Zac outside, talking to Mike as they both leaned against her car. 'Ready?' he asked when he spied her.

She nodded, her mouth still full. Going around to the passenger seat, Julia climbed in and did up her seat belt. She felt intrigued and apprehensive at the same time. After

Zac was settled and had his seat belt on, she glanced at him, hoping for some clue or simply reassurance as to what was going on.

'Zac?' she asked quietly as they pulled out of the driveway and drove down the quiet backstreet Vanessa lived on.

'Hmm?' He looked across at her, his face an unreadable mask.

'Where are we going?'

Zac didn't answer her as he focused on the traffic. She looked out the window at the overcast sky above and then back to the way they were headed. Outside her window, she recognised a group of shops and a school, and she smiled.

'I went to school there.' She pointed and looked at Zac. His jaw was clenched and his hands were gripping the wheel. Something was really worrying him and she had no idea what.

'Please, Zac,' she implored. 'Tell me what's wrong. Where are we going?'

He gently braked at a red light and turned to look at her.

'I'm taking you to meet my wife.'

## CHAPTER NINE

'*WHAT?*' Julia was shocked and stunned. 'Zac, I don't want to meet your wife.'

The light turned green but Zac didn't move. 'You don't understand, Julia. I *need* you to meet my wife.'

The car behind them honked its horn and Zac slowly started driving. Julia was speechless, her mind in utter turmoil. Why did Zac *need* her to meet his ex-wife? Was it so she could see the type of woman who had induced him to matrimony? Obviously Vanessa knew about this and had actually approved.

Her stomach churned as it tied itself into nervous knots and her mouth went dry. She was unable to speak, even if she'd wanted to. Julia shook her head as she gazed out of the window. She frowned. They were pulling into the cemetery.

A dawning realisation hit her with force. Not *once* had Zac referred to Cara as his ex-wife but always as his wife.

'I didn't divorce my wife, Julia,' he said softly, as though he could read her thoughts. He parked the car but remained seated, not turning to look at her. 'She died. Just over three years ago.'

Julia clamped a hand over her mouth as she gasped in shock. 'Oh, Zachary. Oh, I'm so sorry. I had no idea.' She shook her head in disbelief at her honest mistake. Just because *she* was divorced, she'd jumped to the conclusion that Zac had suffered the same fate.

'How could you?' He turned and looked at her, his blue eyes filled with regret. 'Let's go.'

They climbed out of the car, locked it and started walking. Zac took Julia's hand in his, leading the way to a large brick wall that was covered with brass name-plaques. He stopped and raised his hand to one of them, running his fingertips gently across it, as though he was saying hello. Then he stepped back to allow her to read it.

'"Cara Segmüller Carmichael",' she softly read to herself. '"Died on the fourth of November"...' She stopped and looked across at Zac. He was standing with his hands deep in his jeans pockets, his head low as he looked at the ground.

'Zac, we don't have to do this if it causes you too much pain,' she said as she crossed to his side. Julia gently placed her hand on his arm and waited for him to look at her.

He nodded. 'Thanks, Jules, but you, of all people, need to know what happened.'

Julia looked around them and spied a bench beneath a shady tree. 'Why don't we go over there and talk?'

Zac nodded and, without touching, they walked across. Julia wasn't about to push him to start and waited patiently for a few minutes before he spoke.

'Ever since Cara's death, Vanessa has accused me of being more withdrawn, especially during the first year, but that's usually to be expected. I've been trying to break out of that and that's one of the reasons why I let Jeffrey pressure me into that blind date with you.' He smiled for the first time that day. 'I still can't believe it was *you*.'

'What was she like?' Julia forced herself to ask the question, working hard to keep her tone light and friendly.

Zac smiled. 'Cara had short blonde hair and green eyes. She was a general surgeon and we met while we were both overseas, working in one of the emergency hospitals there. She was from Switzerland and right away we hit it off.'

Julia felt her insides twist but forced herself to smile. It was as though she *wanted* to know but *didn't* want to know at the same time. She wanted to be there for Zac to help him move on, but they had to talk about his past first before they could go forward.

'A month after we'd been working together, the revolutionaries started bombing the city where we worked and lived. Things became very intense. The casualties were horrific, the conditions appalling, and my sole motivation when I woke up every morning was to make it through yet another day.

'Cara was the only bright spot in my life, and together we worked and patched people up, long after many of the other staff had returned to their native lands. Then one day Cara was accidentally shot.'

Julia gasped and covered her mouth with her hand.

'She was all right,' he hurried on. 'Sorry. I didn't mean to startle you. The bullet had gone into her back, missing every vital organ. I was able to operate and remove it. The whole ordeal, though, started Cara thinking about everything she'd planned to do with her life, and one of them was to be married. She hadn't expected to die a single woman. She wasn't in any danger of dying from her injury but neither of us knew what tomorrow held. So I decided to surprise her by filing for a special marriage licence. When it came through, we had the local minister to do the honours and we were married.' Zac smiled sadly and gently shook his head.

'We were married for fifteen months when she died—in childbirth.' The last two words were said softly and Julia took a moment to register what he was saying. Zac had a child? This was more than she could fathom. Perhaps she *didn't* know him that well after all. The man who'd decided never to marry and have a family had done just that.

The only problem was, though—where was his child? Julia struggled to find the right words to ask the question, but as she saw Zac's frown deepen she realised he was struggling with his emotions.

She reached out and placed her hand on his. 'Zachary, you don't have to go on. I can see how hard this is for you. Really, let's just leave it—'

'No. I want to tell you. To get it all out in the open.' Zac stood and led her back to the plaques and pointed to the one next to Cara's. 'My daughter's name was Zoe. She was premature and was born at twenty-six weeks.' Julia quickly read the plaque next to Cara's.

'The whole unplanned pregnancy was filled with complications and the labour was no different. Scar tissue from her gunshot wound was the main problem and when that ruptured, she started bleeding badly. Another doctor and I operated on Cara to try and stop the bleeding but we could only do it once Zoe had been born. There were two nurses. One stayed to help us and the other took Zoe.' He shook his head, a tear running silently down his cheek. Julia squeezed his hand with empathy. 'Once Cara was gone, I knew I had to get out of there to at least give Zoe a chance at life. There were no Humidicribs, no specialised equipment to deal with a prem baby, and we simply had to make do with what we had. Somehow, she battled on until we arrived back in Sydney. She was two days old then.

'Even when she was hooked up to all the machines available to help her, the paediatricians didn't give her much hope. When she was ten weeks old, she contracted pneumonia. She never fully recovered. She died at thirteen weeks.'

'Oh, Zac.' Julia closed her eyes for a second and the tears fell over her lashes to trail silently down her cheek. When he touched her face to brush them away, Julia opened her eyes. 'Oh, Zac,' she said again as the tears started to fall more frequently. When *he* sniffed, it was her undoing.

She tugged him closer and wrapped her arms about him, laying her head against his chest. He enveloped her tightly and together they cried for the past. If only she'd stayed with him all those years ago. If only she'd been able to talk him around to marriage, perhaps all of this hurt and pain during the past decade could have been avoided.

But that's not what had happened. She had been married to an awful man and had become a stronger person because of it. She had a gorgeous son who was happy and healthy whilst Zac had married a woman who had died and then a few months later lost his baby girl as well. It wasn't fair. None of it was fair.

Julia remembered Edward when he was born and to have him taken from her, either as a young infant or now…

A fresh bout of tears erupted from her and she held Zac as close as possible. She was crying not only for him but for the pain *any* parent would have felt upon having their baby taken from them in death.

Finally, she raised her head and looked up at him. She hiccuped and he smiled down at her.

'Shall we go?'

Julia looked over at the plaques once more, empathising with Cara for never being able to hold her little girl in her arms. Feeling for Zoe, who would have been so tiny and fragile. Then she returned her attention to the man in her arms. The man who was still alive and living with these memories every day of his life. Not only with the memories of his wife and daughter but also the horrific images from the war-torn country he'd worked in.

The man she loved with all her heart.

'Thank you,' she whispered, and leaned up to kiss him

softly on the lips. There was nothing romantic about it and neither of them pursued it. She nodded. 'Let's go.'

Neither of them spoke much on the drive home but it was a comfortable silence, Zac holding her hand the entire way. When they arrived back at Vanessa's, Edward greeted her enthusiastically at the door, giving his mother a big hug.

Julia held onto him so tightly, so possessively. Her baby.

'Mummy, you hurting me,' he complained, and she loosened her grip, kissing him three times before letting go.

'Are you OK?' Vanessa asked with concern.

Julia nodded. 'Thanks for looking after him.'

'You're welcome. He was no trouble at all.'

Zac excused himself and went upstairs, leaving Julia and Vanessa to stare after him. Julia was worried about him and wondered whether she should go after him.

'Best leave him for a while,' Vanessa said, and Julia looked at her friend. 'I can see that you're concerned—I am, too, but Zac just needs a little space. He'll be fine.'

Julia narrowed her gaze. 'Does this happen often?'

Vanessa nodded and walked through to the kitchen, leaving Julia to follow. 'Kettle's just boiled. Want some tea?'

'Sure.'

Both women were silent while the tea was made and it wasn't until they were sitting outside on the deck that Vanessa said softly, 'Every time he comes here and sees the children, the pain of what he's lost is evident in his eyes. Only for a second,' she added. 'He loves our children and he's very good with them—the perfect uncle.'

Julia agreed. 'He's been great with Edward this weekend.'

'That's not hard. He's adorable,' her friend said sincerely.

Julia smiled but slowly it faded as her thoughts turned once more to Zac's daughter. 'Even to *think* about having Edward taken from me...' She choked, unable to continue, and Vanessa agreed.

'But we can't think like that. Zac has come to terms with his loss but that still doesn't make the emotions any easier to deal with at times.'

They settled into a melancholy silence before being interrupted by the twins. Vanessa went to settle the dispute and while she was gone Zac came out with his own cup of tea.

'How are you doing?' he asked quietly as he sat in the chair his sister had vacated.

Julia smiled. 'I'm more concerned about you.'

'I'm fine.' He smiled as though to prove it. The smile didn't quite reach his eyes.

'Remember who you're talking to, Zac. I can tell when you're lying.'

He nodded and dropped the pretence. 'Listen, Julia,' he said seriously, and she held her breath, knowing he was about to say something serious.

'Mummy! Mummy!' Edward wailed as he came tearing out of the house, headed in her direction. She quickly put her cup on the ground just as he threw himself at her.

'What's wrong?' she asked.

'Dare biting, Mum. Dare biting.'

'Who's fighting?' she asked, but the moment the words were out of her mouth she heard the yells from the twins inside. Next came Vanessa's voice, telling them both to go to their rooms.

'He's not used to other children, especially siblings and the way they...argue,' she explained to Zac, who had a concerned look on his face. 'It's all right, darling.' She cradled Edward in her arms and explained what was happening, not sure that he fully comprehended her words.

Vanessa came out, rolling her eyes and shaking her head. 'Everything's settled,' she told them, and checked that Edward was all right.

That was the last time Julia had all day to be alone with Zac. He'd lost his serious air and was as happy and as charming as he always was. She watched him playing happily with Edward and hope started to grow within her.

When it was time to leave, Julia started to feel a little nervous about being alone with Zac. Should she tell him that she wanted more than just friendship with him? That she was in love with him? She'd come full circle and was now back to wondering whether or not they would have a future together.

They said goodbye to Vanessa and her family, promising to see each other again soon. The drive proceeded in silence and Zac seemed lost in his thoughts.

'I had a fantastic time,' she said, about half an hour into their trip.

'Good.'

Julia checked the back seat and, sure enough, Edward was sound asleep.

'I really appreciate you doing the driving, Zac.'

'No problem. I enjoy it and I really didn't want you hurting your back again.'

'Well, I appreciate that as well.'

He nodded.

'Zac, was there something you were going to say to me back at Vanessa's? This afternoon, before we were interrupted?'

He was silent again and Julia thought he meant to ignore

her, but she wasn't going to let this drop. She wanted whatever it was out in the open.

'You're right. There *is* something I want to say but not while I'm driving. I don't want to risk having an accident.'

'Fair enough,' she said and once more gazed out the window at the passing traffic. 'What do you think about Bianca Hayden?' The silence was unbearable and she needed to talk about *something*. 'Do you think she'll concentrate more on her recovery now that Mona is helping her out?'

'Hopefully.'

They discussed patients and work until they arrived back at Julia's house. Zac switched off the engine and climbed out, not looking at Julia. She followed suit and opened the front door of her house.

'Mum? We're home,' she called, and when she received no reply, she realised there were no lights on in the house. 'Mum?' she called, a little more cautiously. It was just after eight o'clock. Not early enough for her mother to go to bed.

'Do you want me to carry Edward in?' Zac asked, but Julia held up her hand as she strained to listen for *any* sounds coming from within the house.

'Mum?' she called again and ran up the hallway, pushing open her mother's bedroom door. No one was there.

'Maybe she's gone out?' Zac reasoned.

Julia shook her head as an overwhelming sense of dread gripped her. 'No.' She rushed into the kitchen and checked the board where she and her mother left notes for each other. Nothing was written there.

'No,' she said again. 'It's something else. Something has happened.' She reached for the phone and pointed to the door. 'Just keep an eye on Edward in the car, please.'

'Who are you calling?' he asked as he headed for the door. Julia followed him with the cordless phone.

'Jeffrey.' She waited impatiently for him to pick up the phone and then received a message that her call was being redirected. 'Come on,' she said, and told Zac what was happening. Finally he answered. 'Jeffrey, it's Julia.'

'Oh, thank goodness you've called. I've been trying to reach you on your mobile but kept getting your answering service. Zac's phone must be off.'

'Where's Mum?'

'She's here. At the hospital.'

'The *hospital*!' Her eyes were wide with fright as she looked at Zac who was already walking towards the car. 'We're on our way,' she said, and disconnected the call. Slamming her front door shut, Julia sprinted to the car. The instant she was in, Zac started reversing.

'Did he say what was wrong?' Zac asked as Julia pulled her mobile phone from her bag. Sure enough, the battery was flat.

'No. He said that he'd been trying to call both our mobile phones but that neither one was answering. My battery's flat. Where's your phone?'

Zac groaned. 'It's in my bag in the back. It's an unconscious thing that on my weekend off I turn that thing off. I'm a slave to it at every other time of the day and night.'

'You don't need to explain to me,' she snapped, and when he looked across at her she immediately apologised.

'Understood,' he replied, and just when she could have used some reassurance from him, a squeeze of her hand, one of his heart-warming smiles, she got nothing, except safe driving.

Which wasn't to be sneezed at, she reminded herself. She wouldn't do her mother any good if they were involved in a car accident. No, he was right to concentrate on the roads, but still...a small sign of affection would have gone a long way.

Julia glanced into the back of the car to check on Edward—still sound asleep. He'd probably wake when she took him out of the car but it couldn't be helped.

Zac pulled the car into the ambulance parking bay and hurried inside, tossing the car keys to an orderly who would re-park Julia's car. She undid Edward's seat belt, murmuring quiet words to him as she hauled him out and cradled him in her arms. He whimpered and she kissed him.

'It's all right, darling,' she crooned as she headed inside. The big bright lights of A and E made her son blink several times before he finally opened his eyes *and* his mouth to start crying.

'Shh, baby. It's all right,' she crooned again as she hurried towards the treatment rooms. Several of the staff looked at her with surprise. It was obvious they all had no idea whose child she was carrying.

'Is he OK?' Triage sister asked.

'He's fine. I just had to wake him up to take him out of the car. What's going on?'

Zac rounded the corner as she spoke. 'Your mother's in T1, Jules. Here. Give me Edward.' He held out his hands for her son and Julia thought things couldn't be too good if he didn't want her to take Edward in when she saw her mother. 'He'll be fine.'

Julia nodded and kissed her son. 'You go with Zac, darling. Mummy will be back in a minute.'

'Mummy?' she heard the triage sister mumble, but Julia had no time for anyone else, except for the woman who was in treatment room one. Opening the door, she gasped in shock as she saw her mother lying on the bed, a bruise on her face, a cut above her eyebrow and her right shoulder in a sling.

'Oh, Mum,' she gasped softly as she crossed to her mother's side. She kissed her and asked, 'What happened?'

'Read the notes,' Cassandra mumbled, and closed her eyes.

Julia quickly scanned the necessary forms that gave the history of the patient's injuries and how they'd been sustained. 'You were *mugged*?' She couldn't believe it. According to the hospital records, her mother had been leaving the shopping centre and waiting for the bus when a man had attacked her and stolen her handbag. The ambulance and police had been called and Cassandra had been brought to the hospital.

'They've taken very good care of me,' Cassandra said quietly. 'They asked me if I was related to their new Dr Bolton and when I said I was your mother, they contacted Jeffrey immediately.'

Julia nodded. 'Hospital protocol. The head surgeon should be contacted and as Zac wasn't here, Jeffrey is next in line.' She reread her mother's list of injuries. Facial lacerations and bruises and query fractured scapula. They were currently waiting for the radiographs to be processed.

'Jeffrey said he'd get hold of you so I haven't been worried. Where's Edward?'

'He's with Zac.'

'Go and check on him, dear, and put my mind at rest.'

'All right,' she said, and kissed her mother once more. 'You'll be fine.'

'I have no doubt about it,' Cassandra replied and closed her eyes to rest.

Julia wasn't sure where Zac might have taken Edward so she tried the tearoom first. They were in there all right. Zac had Edward firmly on his knee, his big arms around her son, and was playing This Little Piggy Went To Market with one of Edward's feet. Both little shoes were on the floor and Edward was giggling as Zac tickled him.

Julia's heart turned over at the sight of both man and boy laughing, two sets of blue eyes twinkling happily. The two males she loved the most—and here they were, in front of her, enjoying each other's company. Any awkwardness that Zac had initially felt upon learning of Edward's existence two short weeks ago seemed to have vanished. She swallowed the lump that had formed in her throat just as Zac looked up. His smile didn't disappear as she'd thought it would and instead he motioned her in.

'Again. Again,' Edward squealed, and Zac's deep laughter rumbled, causing Julia to smile as well.

'What are you two doing?' she asked as she tickled Edward's tummy. 'And where have your shoes gone, cheeky monkey?'

'Day on da floor,' he told her with another giggle, and pointed downwards.

Julia's heart turned over again with love for Zac. He'd taken Edward, making him happy. That was more than any mother could have asked for, but this had just been one isolated occasion. After her marriage to Ian, Julia had always been sceptical of men and their motives, but with Zac she trusted him implicitly, especially when it came to her son. How could she *not* trust him when she loved him so completely?

'All right, darling,' she said as she took Edward off Zac's knee. 'We'd better get you sorted out.' Her mind raced ahead, knowing she needed someone to look after Edward while she waited here at the hospital for her mother.

'No. I wanna stay wif Zac,' he said, and lunged for the man in question. Julia held her son firmly, which wasn't easy as he kept wriggling. She pulled a chair out and sat down.

'Listen, sweetheart,' she said, 'Grandma had a little accident and she's a bit hurt.'

Edward's eyes grew wide with surprise. 'Gr'ma hurt? Oh, no,' he said, his gaze now displaying worry. Julia kissed his head with love.

'Zac is going to make Grandma all better.' Julia knew without even asking that Zac would be performing any surgery her mother might need to fix the scapula back into position, should it be required. It was against hospital protocol for her to operate or even assist with her mother's treatment.

'So we need to let Zac go and see how Grandma is and then tomorrow, when you've had a good sleep, you can come back and see her.'

'And Zac?' Edward asked, looking at the man beside her.

Julia didn't answer, not knowing whether Zac would want that. After all, they'd both be here tomorrow—Monday. Business as usual. Again her mind was racing. How was she going to care for Edward while her mother was in hospital?

'Of course, mate,' Zac said. 'I'd better go,' he said softly to Julia. 'I'll let you know what's happening.'

'I'd appreciate it,' she replied. Zac turned and headed towards the door. As he did so, Jeffrey walked in.

'Jeffwe,' Edward said excitedly and scrambled off Julia's knee, launching himself at Jeffrey.

'Hello, mate,' Jeffrey said, and picked him up. He looked at Zac. 'You on your way to see Cassandra?'

'Yes.'

'Keep me informed,' he ordered, and Zac left. 'Sorry,' he said as he crossed to Julia's side. 'How are you, scallywag?' He also tickled Edward's tummy and the little boy giggled again. 'I've been held up with the police report but everything seems to be in order now.'

'Thanks, Jeffrey,' Julia said, and kissed his cheek.

'Hey, that's what family's for,' he told her seriously.

'Excuse me,' Triage Sister said from the doorway. 'Sorry to interrupt, but your wife is looking for you, Dr McArthur. Shall I bring her in?'

'Please,' he said with a nod. Moments later Mona came in and it was her turn to have the missile named Edward launched at her.

'Hello, gorgeous,' she said, and bent down to kiss him. She came over and pulled out a chair. Edward scrambled from one person's knee to the next, wanting to tell Mona and Jeffrey everything that had happened on his 'holiday' in Bwisb'ne. They listened intently before Julia found a piece of paper and a pen so that he could do a special drawing for Grandma.

'I don't want you to worry about anything,' Mona told Julia. 'Jeffrey and I have worked everything out.'

'We'll sleep at your place this evening in the guest room. Mona can drive Edward home now, while you and I wait for some results on the operation. Tomorrow, Mona will spend some time with Edward in the morning before bringing him into the hospital so he can see Cassandra.'

'What about Bianca Hayden?' Julia asked.

'I've arranged to spend an hour with her tomorrow,' Mona said.

Jeffrey cut in, 'Right, so while she's doing that, Edward can come up and play in my office.'

Julia gave a grateful smile. 'That's kind of you but I feel terrible about letting him disrupt your routines like this.' Julia didn't usually like people taking charge of her life but for the moment she knew she had to accept the help both Mona and Jeffrey were offering. If it had been anyone else, she would have turned them down flat, but this was Jeffrey and Mona. People who had been there to help and support her from the moment she'd kicked Ian out.

'It's fine, Julia,' Jeffrey told her. 'Don't worry about it.'

'I just need to get through morning clinic and then I can take my paperwork home and finish it there.'

'All right,' he said, and slapped his knee. 'Mona's going to spend the afternoon talking to that fellow from the bus crash so it's all settled.' Jeffrey stood up and puffed out his chest. 'I'm *always* right,' he said proudly.

'And your ego is way too big,' Julia jested.

'Come on, gorgeous,' Mona said as she bent to put Edward's shoes back on. 'I'm going to have a sleepover at *your* house.'

'Wow!' Edward said, and started tugging Mona out of the room.

'Hey, don't I get a kiss goodbye?' Julia asked, but was pleased that Edward seemed so happy with the arrangements.

'Silly-billy me,' Edward said, and Julia laughed at the expression. He gave her a kiss and then another one. 'Dat for Zac,' he said seriously.

'Oh.' Julia tried not to meet Mona's or Jeffrey's gaze as she said, 'I'll make sure he gets it.' She glanced up to see the other adults smiling.

'I'll just bet you do,' Jeffrey murmured, wiggling his eyebrows up and down. He said goodbye to his wife and Edward, and when they were left alone he turned to Julia. 'What's going on between you and Zac?'

'Who knows?' she said, throwing her arms up in the air.

'He has a lot of issues in the past that stop him from entering the present.'

'You mean Cara and Zoe?'

Jeffrey seemed surprised. 'He told you?'

Julia nodded. 'He took me to the cemetery this morning.'

'Whew! You *have* had a busy day.'

'It's been an emotional roller-coaster but I have the funny feeling that the ride isn't over yet.'

'Hang in there,' Jeffrey advised. 'The fact that he's confided in you so soon means a lot, Julia.'

'I know, but there's something more coming. I don't know what.' She shrugged. 'Woman's intuition, I guess. Just like I knew something was wrong with Mum the instant I walked into the house tonight.'

'Don't you worry about Cassandra. That woman is as strong as steel. She'll be fine.' Jeffrey tenderly placed his arm around her shoulders. Julia rested her head against him and sighed. She wished it were Zac holding her, Zac offering his comfort, Zac taking charge.

'I know.'

'And don't worry about Zac. No matter what happens, I know you two will work things out.' Julia must have looked dubious because he smiled at her and said, 'Trust me.'

As it turned out, Cassandra did need surgery on her shoulder. 'It's basic and straightforward,' Zac said as he showed Julia and Jeffrey the X-rays.

'How long will it take?' Jeffrey asked.

'About forty-five minutes.' He took the radiographs down and returned them to the packet. 'She's about to have her pre-med so if you want to go and talk to her, now's the time.' Again Julia was getting the cold shoulder from Zac. There was definitely something wrong but *what*?

Julia went to see her mother and gave her a kiss as the anaesthetist came in. She stayed with Cassandra until they were ready to take her into Theatre. Feeling helpless, she returned to the tearoom to wait with Jeffrey.

Thankfully, the time didn't pass too slowly and all too soon Zac was standing before them, a satisfied look on his face. 'She's in Recovery,' he told her, and Julia smiled.

'Thank you,' she said, and regardless of whether or not he wanted her to touch him, she gave him a hug. 'Thank you, Zac.'

'Go see her,' he advised, and Julia did just that. Cassandra looked fine and Julia eagerly read the operation notes that had been written in Zac's handwriting. He'd always had quite neat and legible handwriting, which, for a doctor, was fairly rare. She smiled to herself as she remembered the countless times people had asked her to decipher her own scrawl. Nine times out of ten, *she* hadn't even been able to do it!

'He's wonderful,' Cassandra murmured as Julia quickly crossed to her mother's side.

'Hi. Are you feeling any pain?'

'Ooh, no. Just as fine as fine can be. That Zac is a charmer,' she told Julia with a silly schoolgirl grin on her face.

'So I've noticed. I never thought he'd get you, though,' she confessed.

'Sorry, dear, but he has. I like him a lot and would be more than proud to call him my son-in-law.'

'Whoa, Mum. You're jumping the gun here.'

'You will be. He loves you, Julia. I'm sure of it.'

'It's the medication talking,' Julia rationalised. What was with everyone tonight? First Jeffrey and now her mother. Both declaring a happy and solid future for Zac and herself.

Cassandra mumbled something else that wasn't quite coherent and Julia realised that she'd slipped back into a peaceful slumber. 'I'd better get home to Edward,' she whispered. 'I'll be back to see you tomorrow morning. I love you, Mum.'

'Huh? Oh, yes. Love you, too, dear. Kiss Edward for me.' Cassandra roused, her speech slurred. Nevertheless, the words had been said and Julia felt better. It was nice to know she had people around her who loved and cared for her, but how she desperately wanted Zac to be one of them.

Right now, she was exhausted. She arranged for Jeffrey to take her home and for Zac to keep her car.

'We can swap back tomorrow,' she told him, a mischievous gleam in her eyes. He smiled—a real smile. The first one she'd seen for what seemed like an eternity.

'You just want a chance to drive my Jag, don't you?'

'You'd better believe it. Night, Zac.' She blew him a kiss and laughed as she and Jeffrey walked out the door. It was a nice way to end the night and she realised that just a small, genuine smile from him did *so* much for her. Ah, such was love.

# CHAPTER TEN

THE next morning, Julia arrived at the hospital bright and early, driving Zac's Jaguar, oh, so carefully. She parked it in the doctors' car park next to her own car, which looked like a sensible family car compared to Zac's two seater, soft top. Even in the choice of their cars, they seemed to be at opposite ends of the spectrum. Was that how it was always going to be?

She shook her head and went inside to see her mother before the ward round began.

'How are you feeling?'

'As though I've been hit by a truck.'

Julia smiled. 'Edward made you this,' she said as she pulled a picture from her briefcase. 'Mona will bring him around to see you later this morning. I've got ward round and then clinic.'

'And this afternoon?' Cassandra asked as she accepted the colourful picture her grandson had drawn.

'Paperwork. I can do that at home.'

'I feel so awful about this, dear.'

'Mum, it couldn't have been helped.'

'I suppose I could have driven Zac's car to the shops but it just didn't feel right and, besides, it's not that far on the bus. Only ten minutes. It was just…just…' Tears sprang into Cassandra's eyes and Julia was stunned. She hadn't seen her mother cry since her father's death. It took a lot to faze Cassandra Bolton yet, seeing her like this, Julia realised that her mother was a lot more shaken up than she had previously led her to believe.

'Oh, Mum.' Julia hugged her mother on the left side and gave her a kiss. 'We'll get through this. None of this is your fault. We'll be fine. We always have been.'

'Sorry to interrupt, Julia,' Tess said quietly from behind her. 'The rest of the staff have gathered in the ward briefing room and are waiting for you.'

'Thanks, Tess,' Julia replied, and dabbed at her eyes with a tissue.

'Off you go, dear. I want to rest a bit before the ward round gets to me. All those prying eyes—ugh.' Cassandra shuddered.

Julia smiled. 'You'll be fine.'

Julia entered the briefing room and put her bag and briefcase in the corner. She glanced up at Zac and realised he was staring at her legs. She'd worn a cream skirt today, with a navy silk shirt and a matching cream vest. She'd dressed purely for Zac, knowing he'd always liked her legs.

His gaze flicked to meet hers as she straightened, but he merely nodded and began the briefing. During ward round he was the consummate professional and Julia followed his example. The feeling she'd had last night that something wasn't right still irked her, but she brushed it aside until they were finished.

Aki was slowly progressing and Julia felt it wouldn't be too much longer before they knew what was troubling him. Bianca Hayden, on the other hand, was a changed woman. She was more co-operative and working hard at her rehabilitation. Medically, her pelvis was stabilised and healing nicely with no complications.

'Ah, the magic of Mona,' Julia said after they left Bianca's room and headed up to clinic. She took her bag and briefcase with her, telling herself to remember to swap keys with Zac.

The clinic was full and absolutely hectic. Timmy Jones, the seven-year-old boy who'd fractured his arm, came into the clinic and was reviewed by Zac. He called Julia over as Timmy had brought some more of his cars in for her to see. She spent a few minutes chatting with him and admiring his cars before it was time for him to go.

'That's what I like to see,' she said once the boy had gone. 'Young children without a fear of doctors or hospitals.'

'Agreed.' Zac didn't say anything more, so Julia turned and left.

Dorothy stopped Julia as she came out to ask her a question about a patient. When they were done, the clinic sister said, 'I understand from Zac that you and your son spent the weekend with Vanessa. Did you have a good time?'

'Oh, it was fantastic, seeing her again. She hasn't changed a bit.' Julia didn't miss the reference to her son. After last night, when she'd come into A and E with Edward, she had expected this.

'Good. I'm glad.' Dorothy nodded, and when she didn't move Julia frowned.

'Something else?'

'I had no idea you had a son,' Dorothy said softly. 'And are you *really* related to Jeffrey McArthur?'

Julia's frown disappeared and she smiled. 'I see the grapevine has been hard at work. Yes, I have a son. His name is Edward and he's three years old. As for the other matter, well, Jeffrey and I are *kind* of related but not really.'

It was Dorothy's turn to frown. 'I don't follow.'

'My ex-husband is Jeffrey's cousin.'

'I see.' Dorothy nodded slowly. 'So there's...no...*man* in your life?'

'Ah. That's what the problem is. Just because I have a

child, it automatically means I'm married. Well, no. I'm divorced. I'm a single, working mother. That's all there is to it.'

'How does Zac feel about this?' Dorothy had lowered her voice considerably.

'It shouldn't be anyone's business how Zac feels.'

'Oh, Julia. Believe me, the hospital is on tenterhooks, wondering when that man will get married and settle down. Of course, there have been rumours that he's already been married.' The clinic sister eyed her hopefully and Dorothy shrank dramatically in Julia's opinion. 'I don't suppose you know anything about that?'

'All I know is,' Julia said as she took another file off the stack of case-notes, 'that I'm ready for my next patient. Show them in, please.' She walked off, hoping that Dorothy would get the message!

Once she'd seen her last patient, Julia returned to her office to quickly pack her bag. She'd told Jeffrey that she'd pick Edward up as soon as clinic had finished.

There was a tap at her door and Julia looked up. Zac's secretary poked her head around. 'Hi, Julia.'

'What's up?'

'Zac would like to see you in five minutes if that suits you.'

Oh, gosh—his keys. She'd forgotten again. Julia consulted her watch as she took his keys from her bag. She was already fifteen minutes behind schedule, but what was another five? 'Sure,' she replied, and the secretary left. Julia quickly rang Jeffrey's office to let him know.

'Of course you must see Zac. Edward's fine,' he said. 'Get yourself some lunch from the cafeteria before coming here. I know you too well, Julia Bolton, and chances are you probably won't get around to eating lunch today.'

'Probably,' she agreed. 'Thanks, Jeffrey. I shouldn't be too much longer.'

She raced to the cafeteria and bought a salad roll, which she tossed into her briefcase before going to Zac's office.

'He's just finishing off a meeting with a registrar,' his secretary told her. 'Just knock and go right in. He's expecting you.'

Julia did as she was told.

'Promise me you'll think carefully about everything I've said,' Zac was saying to the registrar who was sitting opposite him. He didn't look up or acknowledge her. 'I admire your dedication and drive but you've got to know and accept the risks of working in a Third World country. Promise me you'll think about it again.'

The registrar promised.

'Good. We'll talk in a few weeks' time.' With that, he dismissed the registrar, who walked past Julia with only a brief nod.

'Everything all right?' she asked. Now that she knew about Zac's past, she could understand his cautionary words to the young doctor.

'Close the door, please,' he said, and waited for her to do just that. Zac stood and walked towards her. His action surprised Julia and she stopped in the middle of the room, unsure what was going to happen next.

'You wanted to see me?' she asked. He was standing close. *Very* close. The scent of his cologne teased at her senses and Julia felt her heart rate increase.

'Uh-huh.' He gazed down at her. It was the old magic that she saw in his eyes. The unmistakable look of desire. Her breathing became rapid and she parted her lips, surprised at his attitude but not willing to stop it.

Slowly his hands caressed her arms, sliding up and down and up and down. Julia closed her eyes and sighed.

She felt herself begin to sway as his hands cupped her face. Ever so slightly, Zac brushed his lips against hers and Julia groaned with wanting.

'You're very beautiful,' he told her, and dropped his hands. Julia opened her eyes, completely confused, and watched as he took a step away.

'Zachary?'

For five, long, excruciatingly slow seconds, neither of them moved. The world seemed to stand still and then all of a sudden Julia found herself being hauled against him, his mouth pressed firmly to hers in one swift movement.

Julia wasn't about to pass this opportunity up. As far as she was concerned, it had been far too long since Zac had kissed her, and who knew when the next one would be? She wound her arms about his neck and matched his passion.

When he pulled back to look down into her eyes, his breathing was as uneven as her own. She wasn't sure what he was looking for but he'd obviously found it as he returned his mouth to hers once more. This time, though, his mouth moved over hers at a more sedate pace, teasing yet testing.

Julia's knees started to buckle and her head began to swoon as the drug she called Zac filled her senses. His arms tightened, holding her against him, and she was grateful for his support.

Finally, when they parted, Julia rested her head on his chest, panting as though she'd just run a marathon.

'It's so...intense,' he groaned.

'Mmm,' she agreed, unable to form whole words. He continued to hold her until she at last felt as though her legs would support her weight again. Julia edged back and looked up at him. 'You look so sexy when your hair is all ruffled like that,' she whispered.

Zac crushed her to him and groaned. 'When you say things like that, it only makes me want to kiss you some more.'

Julia gazed at him in complete surprise. 'Zac?'

He put her from him and walked to his desk. 'This past weekend with Vanessa was…fun, Jules. It's the first time in, well, years since I've felt that…happy. Telling you about my family was good for me. It's helped to lay a lot of inner turmoil to rest.'

'Oh, Zac…' She took a few steps towards him but he held up his hand.

'It has also made the…areas quite hazy. Working professionally with you. Cara and Zoe. Edward. I'm not sure that everything…' He clasped his hands together, his fingers interlocking.

'Fits together' she finished with a nod.

'Therefore, I'd like to ask you a favour.'

'Name it.' Julia couldn't believe what she was hearing.

'I need a few days, just to think things through. I've spoken to Jeffrey and he's agreed to giving me the next three days off. One of the orthopods from Brisbane is going to come and help out during that time.'

If Julia had been surprised before, it was nothing compared to now. She simply stared at him. Zac smiled slightly and nodded.

'I know what you're thinking. Ten years ago we went our separate ways because I didn't give it enough thought. Well, I'm not going to make the same mistake twice, Julia. Give me the next few days and on Friday night I'd like the two of us to go out to dinner.'

'You mean…like a…*date*?'

His smile increased at her incredulity. 'Yes, Jules.'

'Well…all right, then.' The phone on his desk shrilled to life but he made no move to pick it up. It was enough, however, to snap Julia out of her amazement. 'I'll let you get that and I'll...um...see you.'

'Wait,' he said, and snatched the receiver up. 'Zac Carmichael. Already?' He listened. 'Give me five minutes.' He hung the phone up and walked towards her. 'I have a meeting to get to.'

'Oh, and I have Jeffrey and Edward waiting. I'd completely forgotten.'

'So...' Zac placed his hands on her shoulders. 'I'll see you on Friday?'

Julia smiled up at him and nodded. 'Most definitely.'

He pressed his lips firmly to hers but not for too long. 'Get going,' he said as he took a step back. 'You're too tempting for words.'

Julia laughed, feeling light-headed and giddy. She turned and headed for the door before stopping and looking at him once more. 'I almost forgot.' She reached into her pocket and pulled out his car keys.

'Thanks.' As they swapped keys, Zac took the opportunity to kiss her once more before saying, 'Go, or we'll never leave this office!'

'Sounds promising,' she teased, unable to believe what had transpired. Zac was willing to give them a chance! It was promising that now he was going to do just that. Taking three days off work was a *big* thing for him and the sentiment wasn't lost on her at all. Also, he wanted them to go on a date. Another big step for him. Julia shook her head, trying not to allow rational thought to intrude into her romantic haze.

The silly, happy grin refused to leave her face as she walked to Jeffrey's office. When she arrived, as usual the sight of her son only increased her happiness.

'Mummy!' he exclaimed, and she dropped everything and opened her arms wide to envelop him in a hug.

'Mmm, you're just what Mummy needs to top things off,' she told him, and hugged him close.

'You're certainly happy,' Jeffrey said, his own smile wide. 'So what did Zac want to see you about?'

'As if you didn't know,' she teased. Julia kissed his cheek. 'Thank you for pulling some strings and organising these days off for him. That means a lot to me and I'm sure to Zac as well.'

'My pleasure,' Jeffrey replied.

The three days without Zac were absolute agony. Julia couldn't believe how long a day could be as they seemed to stretch on for ever. Combined with that was the gossip around the hospital at Zac's sudden departure. Several staff asked Julia questions but she simply shrugged and told them to ask Jeffrey or Zac if they really wanted answers, knowing none of them ever would!

The time also helped Julia's doubts to return in force and fester, until by Thursday night she could hardly sleep. She knew Zac needed the time and she was glad he was taking it. He'd been open and honest with her, just as he'd been in the past. Yet what if he once more decided that he didn't want to pursue family life again? He'd asked her out on a date but perhaps that was simply to tell her of the decision he'd reached. Would he risk accepting a ready-made family? Would he risk loving her again?

By Friday morning, she was a nervous wreck and anxiously awaiting his return. Zac had appeared for ward round but only seconds before it had started, so she'd had no time to talk to him.

He'd neither smiled nor frowned at her and she was now too exhausted to read his body language accurately. After ward round, she'd promised Edward they'd spend some time with Cassandra.

'Watch me, Gr'ma,' Edward said.

'I'm watching.' Cassandra waited patiently for her grandson. Edward stood on the floor and, concentrating very hard, did a hop. 'Oh, clever boy,' Cassandra praised.

'He was practising all yesterday afternoon,' Julia told her mother, and they both smiled. Edward had brought such happiness into their lives.

'There you are,' Mona said as she walked across to Cassandra's bed. 'Julia, I've found out what's wrong with Aki.'

'What?' Julia's eyes were wide with surprise. 'Great. Let's call Zac and have him meet us.' She stood and looked at her mother, then at Edward. 'I'll take him.'

'No,' Cassandra protested, and switched on the television set. 'If you'll lift him up onto the bed, we can snuggle together and watch some TV.'

Julia did as her mother asked, telling her son not to move or he might hurt Grandma. 'Back soon,' she told him, and hurried over to the men's ward with Mona. She stopped at the nurses' station and paged Zac. Mona refused to say a word until Zac had arrived.

'What is it?' Zac asked eagerly. Julia could tell that whatever was happening between them on a personal level had nothing to do with what was happening with their patients. She looked at Mona and concentrated on what she was about to say. The sooner they found out what was *really* bothering their patient, the sooner they'd be able to fix it.

'I was right with my earlier hunch. He *has* lost face.'

'Because he was injured in a bus accident?' Zac couldn't believe it.

'No.' Mona shook her head. 'It's because of his asthma.'

'Why?'

'To his people, asthma is seen as a disability.'

'Surely not?' Julia found this difficult to believe.

'I'm afraid so, dear. Aki feels he has brought shame not only on himself but on his family name as well. To have an attack in public, as he did on the tour bus, has been most shameful to him.'

'Doesn't he realise that there are a lot of people who suffer from asthma?' Zac asked.

'Why don't we go and talk to him?' Mona suggested. 'Let him know that things aren't as bad as they seem.'

'Sounds like a great idea,' Julia said, and gave Mona a hug. 'I knew you'd sort everything out. You're a very special woman, Mona McArthur.'

'Thank you, dear.' Mona smiled brightly at them both before they headed over to Aki's bed to talk to him. Mona translated everything they said and by the time they left Aki had a smile on his face for the first time.

When she returned to her mother's bedside, Edward was curled up on her mother's uninjured side, watching television without a fuss. She bent to give him a kiss but he was too engrossed to notice.

Julia smiled to herself and sat down in the chair by the bed. She glanced over her shoulder to the doorway to the female ward, and found herself looking into Zac's hypnotic blue gaze. Her smile disappeared as desire, mixed with longing, began to burn deep within her. They had a few more hours to get through before all would be revealed.

That night, Julia dressed with care. She wore a cream dress that ended at mid-thigh, and had inch-thick straps. She left her hair loose, just for Zac. When the doorbell rang, her heart was hammering wildly against her ribs and her mouth was dry.

'Hi,' she breathed as she opened the door. He looked incredible, dressed in black trousers and a chambray shirt.

They drank their fill of each other before he pulled a large bunch of frangipani out from behind his back.

'Oh, Zac. They're beautiful,' she said as she took them from him. 'You remembered.' She gazed at him, revelling in his smile.

'Ready?'

'I'll just say goodnight to Mona.'

'Where's Edward?' he asked, looking around.

'Asleep.' She carried the flowers into the kitchen, *feeling* Zac follow her rather than seeing him.

'Oh, aren't they lovely?' Mona smiled at Zac. 'Let me put them in some water for you, dear, so you two can get going.'

'Thanks.' Julia said.

Soon they were riding in Zac's Jaguar to a small, secluded restaurant by the beach. They spoke of their patients during the drive and discussed hospital protocols during dinner. Julia started to wonder whether this was a promising sign or not!

'Zac?' He looked up from his coffee and smiled. Her heart turned over with love for him and she silently prayed that tonight wasn't going to be the beginning of the end. 'H-how were the last…um…three days?'

His smiled increased. 'Why? Did you miss me?'

'Terribly,' she confessed in a whisper.

'I missed you, too.'

This was good, she thought. A very good beginning. 'So are you going to keep me in suspense any longer?'

'Maybe.' He shrugged and then laughed. 'I did a lot of thinking after retreating into my cave—not literally, you understand,' he added. 'And I think we should…seriously date. I need to spend time with Edward as well as time with you. I really missed you, Julia.' He reached out and took her hand in his across the table.

It was more than Julia had secretly hoped for. She *did* notice that he hadn't suggested marriage or any permanent relationship but still...it was definitely a step forward.

For the next week they did just that, with each date ending with a chaste goodnight kiss. Zac obviously wanted to take things slowly...*very* slowly...and Julia wasn't about to argue. It was important for Edward to feel as comfortable with Zac as she did. During Zac's visits they played cars and trucks, as well as running around outside and playing with a football.

Edward was definitely becoming attached to Zac and that in itself caused Julia happiness as well as apprehension. What if she and Zac *didn't* end up together? What if Zac was happy to date Julia, but not to marry her, as he'd done in the past? Zac had never offered to have Edward by himself and Julia wasn't sure she wanted to encourage it—at this stage. Perhaps in the future...

Near the end of that week, Zac received a phone call from Jeffrey. 'I have a problem,' his friend said.

'What's up?'

'I told Julia I'd look after Edward tomorrow afternoon but I've just had a meeting scheduled with the State Minister for Health and I can't possibly cancel. I know you usually tackle your paperwork on Friday afternoon, so would you mind doing it from home and watching Edward while Julia's operating?'

Zac had realised that Julia hadn't suggested that he and Edward spend time together without her, and wasn't sure how she'd feel about this arrangement. 'Ah—what about Mona?'

'She'll be working with Bianca Hayden.'

'And Cassandra?'

'She has her physio appointment. She can't miss that. You're her doctor, you should know that.'

'I do. Isn't there anyone else? A day-care centre?'

'Julia can't get him in until Monday. They don't take children at such short notice. Honestly, Zac, if it was anyone but the Minister I'd cancel, but you realise how important this meeting is.'

'I thought you weren't supposed to meet the Minister until next week.'

'I was, but he had a cancellation and I got moved up in the queue.'

'Are you sure there isn't anyone else?'

'No one. Why the hesitation? I thought you and Julia were a couple now.'

'We're dating, Jeffrey. Getting to know each other again.' He raked a hand through his hair. 'How does Julia feel about this?' There was silence on the end of the line and Zac began to feel even more uneasy. 'She doesn't know, does she? You're organising her son for her without asking her permission.'

'Look, Zac, if I tell Julia I can't look after him, she'll have to cancel her operating list. Do you know how much money that will cost the hospital? I can't leave Edward with just *anyone*, and he knows you. He can't stop talking about you.'

'Yeah, he's a great kid.' Zac closed his eyes and Edward's image came readily into his mind. He liked the little guy and really wanted to help out, but still wasn't sure how he felt about going behind Julia's back. He wanted to help Julia. 'All right,' Zac agreed. 'But only on the condition that Julia knows I'm looking after him and is OK with it. I won't have you organising this behind her back.'

'Fair enough.' They sorted out the details, with Jeffrey

promising to ring Julia the instant he hung up from Zac. 'Thanks, mate.'

Zac sat back and took a deep breath, a smile on his face as he planned what he and Edward would do the next day. Three whole hours, alone with Julia's son. It made him feel very happy.

'You did *what*?' Julia couldn't believe what she was hearing.

'I've asked Zac to take Edward tomorrow afternoon.' Jeffrey said down the phone. 'What's the problem? I thought you two were a couple?'

'We're *dating*, Jeffrey. It doesn't mean he wants to get married.'

'Ah, so *that's* what's bothering you. Look, Zac has spent time with Edward and there's just no one free to look after him during your operating list tomorrow.'

'I know, I know,' Julia said, feeling churlish. 'You and Mona have been so great this past week. I'm sorry, Jeffrey. It's just...this will be the first time Zac's been alone with Edward and I'm not sure what will happen.'

'Oh, come on. Edward is a wonderful child.'

'He hasn't been sleeping too well since Mum's accident. His little world has been turned upside down. What if he throws a tantrum?'

'They're few and far between. Besides, I'm sure Zac will cope.'

'But what if it turns him off?'

'Ah, I see. That's where you're coming from. Julia, darling, there comes a time when you're just going to have to trust the two of them together. You know them both, you love them both—so just take the step.'

'You're right.'

'Aren't I always?'

Julia laughed. 'Thanks for organising this for me. So you'll drop him off?'

'Zac will pick him up from my office at two o'clock and take him back to his place. You can pick him up when you're finished in Theatre.'

It was all organised.

Julia was on edge during ward round the next day, and when they were done she touched Zac's arm and waited for him to look at her. When he did, her heart turned over with love.

'Thanks for having Edward this afternoon. I really appreciate it.'

'You're more than welcome. Actually, I'm looking forward to it.' He smiled and patted her hand. 'Good news about Aki.'

'The best. Now that we know what's wrong, it's good to see him looking happier.'

When she started her list that afternoon, she had a hard time trying not to think about Zac and Edward together. What were they doing? Were they having fun? Was Zac coping?

She shook her head and finished scrubbing. 'Focus,' she whispered, and closed her eyes for a moment before opening them and heading into Theatre, her mind geared for the operation ahead.

Exactly three hours later, she walked out of Theatres, wrote up the notes and headed for the changing rooms. After changing, Julia had to stop herself from racing from the hospital to see how Zac and Edward were getting along. She hadn't been paged, so nothing major had obviously happened. She headed to Recovery to check on her patients before she left.

Finally, she walked out to the car park and looked at

the address Jeffrey had given her before heading to Zac's apartment.

The traffic was awful and Julia started to seethe impatiently, but still drove safely and took her time. Eventually, she was in the high-powered lift, riding her way up to Zac's luxury serviced apartment. *Another* difference between them. Not only their cars symbolised their priorities but their accommodation did as well. She had the roomy four-bedroom home and Zac had his high-rise apartment.

She stood outside the door, her heart hammering wildly against her chest and her breathing slightly erratic. She closed her eyes, willing herself to relax, and gave her arms a little shake. She knocked on the door and a moment later heard a squeal of excitement.

'Mummy! My mummy's here.'

Zac opened the door, a wide smile on his face, and the breath Julia had been unconsciously holding whooshed out at the sight of him. He was wearing an old pair of jeans that fitted him to perfection and an old Brisbane University T-shirt. He looked more like a beach-bum than an orthopaedic surgeon, but to Julia he'd never looked more handsome. Edward lunged at her legs, nearly knocking her down. Zac reached out a hand to steady her and Julia tingled at his touch.

'Hi, there,' he said, and welcomed her in. She managed to disentangle Edward's arms from her legs, only to have her son pull her into the room, talking so fast with excitement that she couldn't understand him. She bent down to hug him but he was too absorbed in telling her everything that had happened.

She caught the words 'beach', 'sandcastle', 'shops' and '*cars*'. As he said the last word, his entire face lit up in awe. 'Wow,' Julia replied, still unsure what her son was talking about but knowing he was waiting for her response.

She glanced at Zac and found him leaning against the wall, his hands in his pockets and smiling at her son.

'Look, Mummy. Look.' Edward showed her his prized possession. 'A *new* car.'

Julia looked at Zac and he shrugged.

'A remote-controlled car. Just what we needed,' she told her son, and shook her head in bemusement. Boys and their toys!

Edward became absorbed in it and Julia crossed to Zac. 'Thank you for having him this afternoon.' She leaned forward and accepted his kiss.

'He's been no trouble. In fact...' He paused and smiled. 'I've had a good time. He's been a great help.'

Julia almost sighed with relief. Zac was happy with her son. Edward was happy with Zac. Perhaps there *would* be a happy ending for them all. 'I take it you didn't get your paperwork done?'

He shrugged. 'It'll wait for another day.'

She nodded, knowing the feeling well. They both looked at Edward who was lying down on the floor next to the car, having a conversation with it and doing both voices.

'Well, I guess we'd better give you back your solitude,' she said, not wanting to prolong their stay. She crossed to Edward's bag and made sure everything was in it.

'Actually, I've decided to forgo solitude this evening.' He pushed off the wall and came to stand beside her.

'Oh?'

'I'm coming to your place for dinner.'

She gaped at him and only realised her jaw had dropped open when he leaned over and gently pushed it closed. 'Ah... You're... Did I just...?' She stopped, knowing there was no way she'd get her words out properly with him standing so close. He smelled too good to be true and his attitude towards her seemed almost...flirtatious. *What* had happened today with Edward?

'I've ordered dinner for the six of us and it's due to be delivered to your house in about...' he consulted his watch '...fifteen minutes, so we'd better get a move on.'

'Hold on. For the *six* of us?'

'Yeah. Mona, Jeffrey, your mother and us.' He gestured to the two of them and Edward. 'We've all had a busy day and, well...I'm taking over.'

'Just like that?'

'Fifteen minutes until the food arrives at your house,' he persisted, and took Edward's bag from her. 'Hey, Edward? Why don't we take your new car home and show Jeffrey?'

'Yeah,' Edward replied, still hyped-up with excitement. Julia sighed. So much for getting him to bed at a reasonable hour. Nevertheless, she would have Zac at her place for dinner to compensate for it.

Before she knew it, she was driving to her house with a chattering three-year-old in the back of the car, with Zac following behind in his Jaguar. When she arrived, Jeffrey's car was already parked at the kerb and Julia grimaced, knowing full well she'd left her house in a complete mess that morning.

No sooner had they gone inside and said hello to everyone than the doorbell rang with the delivery of their dinner. Julia glanced around the house and realised it was a lot tidier than when she'd left that morning. She looked at Mona, who was in the kitchen making a pot of tea. Yes, Mona's magic had definitely swept through her house.

Dinner was a casual yet friendly affair as they all ate and talked animatedly. Edward went and found the car Jeffrey had given him the other week and together they all had fun, with Jeffrey and Zac having races up and down the hallway. Edward was laughing and enjoying himself immensely and she didn't have the heart to put him to bed.

'He'll settle down next week,' Cassandra said as she came over to where Julia was watching them race.

'How was the physio today?'

Cassandra shrugged. 'So-so. How was Theatre?'

Julia shrugged. 'So-so. Patients are fine.'

'How are you?' her mother probed.

'All right. How about another cup of tea? Anyone for tea?' she asked, and received affirmative replies.

'I'll get it, dear,' Mona said, but Julia cut her off.

'No. Sit down and relax, Mona. You've already helped me far too much this week. Let me at least make you a cup of tea!' Julia headed into the kitchen and switched the kettle on. She heard a shout of laughter from the other room and smiled. At least everyone was happy.

She yawned and stretched, then jumped in fright as she felt Edward's car hit the back of her heel. 'Ow,' she said, but didn't turn around. 'Be careful, Edward. Mummy's making tea. It's hot. Out of the kitchen, please.' The kettle had boiled so she poured the water into the pot. The car hit her heel again. 'Edward!' She turned around, her gaze going downward to where her son was supposed to be—but he wasn't there. Instead, she was looking at Zac's denim-clad legs. She raised her gaze and looked at him. 'Sorry. I thought it was Edward.'

Zac butted the car against her heel once more and she shifted. 'That hurts, Zac.' She bent down to pick up the car and stopped in mid-bend and froze. There, secured to the top of the antenna of the car, was a diamond ring. She straightened and gasped, her hand over her mouth as her gaze met Zac's.

He crossed to her side and removed her hand. 'Marry me,' he said, and bent his head to kiss her lips. Julia sighed into him, winding her arms about his neck, holding his head firmly in place. She closed her eyes, savouring the way he felt, the way he tasted and the way he made her feel.

Cherished. Adored. *Loved.*

The kiss turned slow and sensual, rocking her to the very core. His tongue gently traced the outline of her lips, lips that trembled slightly beneath his caress before he pressed his mouth back to hers.

She heard the door to the kitchen close but it was inconsequential when Zac was in her arms and her heart was filled with love.

'Julia,' he said when they finally broke apart, 'your son is amazing. I'm so proud of the job you've done of raising him, but it's only going to get harder and I want to be a part of it.'

Julia waited. Waited for him to say more.

'Today, while I was playing with him, I realised how much fun I was having. Spending time with you, dating you, has made me feel alive—truly alive—for the first time since Cara and Zoe died. I want to be a part of your life. You *and* Edward. You make me happy, Julia. You make me think. You make me *feel*, full stop.'

Julia was amazed at what he was saying. Her emotions were moved and she was so desperately filled with love for him that she found herself speechless.

'Julia Louise Bolton, I love you. I always have and I always will. The last time you left, it took me years to get over it, even though I kept telling myself it was what I'd wanted. I'm not going to make that same mistake again. I need you in my life. I need to be your husband and I need to be Edward's father. I want paradise, Julia, and you're the only person who can give it to me.' He pressed his lips to hers as though to prove it.

He broke away momentarily and picked up the car, placing it on the bench. He took the ring off the antenna and slipped it onto the third finger of her left hand. 'Marry me?' he said again.

Tears filled Julia's eyes and she bit her lower lip. Her throat was choked up with emotion so she nodded. 'Yes,' she finally whispered, only to have her mouth crushed against his in a powerfully possessive kiss.

'You're so beautiful,' he murmured moments later as he kissed her neck before looking at her. 'Marry me soon, Julia.'

'As soon as you like.' She smiled, with pure happiness in her heart.

'We should tell the others,' Zac whispered.

'I think they already have a good idea of what's going on in here. Someone's shut the kitchen door to give us a bit of privacy.'

'Oh. Well, then, we should call Vanessa.'

'Soon.' She kissed him again and he didn't argue.

When they came back up for air, he said, 'Let's go show everyone the ring. Edward helped me choose it, you know.'

'Really? Oh, Zac. I love you.' Julia kissed him. 'You're the best. Thank you. That was really sweet of you. Even though I'm sure he doesn't completely understand, thank you for including him.'

'Hey, us males have to stick together.'

'Can we come in yet?' Jeffrey asked through the door.

'Come on in,' Zac said, kissing Julia quickly before everyone came rushing into the kitchen.

'Well, it's about time,' Jeffrey said after Julia and Zac had declared their news. 'I *knew* you two would be perfect for each other.'

Zac and Julia laughed as Zac picked up Edward, including him in their hug. They were going to be a family. At last! Zac kissed Julia—in front of everyone.

'I knew it,' Jeffrey said again.

'And as you know…' Mona laughed. 'My Jeffrey is *always* right!'

Zac kissed Julia again, happier than he'd ever been, knowing that the woman beside him *and* her son were *just* as happy. 'Now, how can we argue with that?'

**Modern Romance™**
...seduction and
passion guaranteed

**Tender Romance™**
...love affairs that
last a lifetime

**Sensual Romance™**
...sassy, sexy and
seductive

*Blaze*
...sultry days and
steamy nights

**Medical Romance™**
...medical drama on
the pulse

**Historical Romance™**
...rich, vivid and
passionate

*29 new titles every month.*

*With all kinds of Romance for
every kind of mood...*

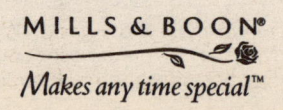

MILLS & BOON®
*Makes any time special*™

MAT4

## MILLS & BOON

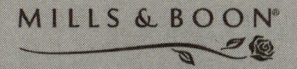

# Medical Romance™

### A WOMAN WORTH WAITING FOR
### by Meredith Webber

*Dr Detective – Down Under*

After five years Ginny is still the beautiful, caring woman Max remembers, and a wonderful emergency nurse. But she clearly hasn't forgiven him. It takes a murder investigation to bring them together, and in their new-found closeness, Max knows that he'd wait for this woman for ever…

### A NURSE'S COURAGE by Jessica Matthews

*Part 3 of Nurses Who Dare*

ER nurse Rachel Wyman has come back to Hooper to think about a new career. But Nick Sheridan adores Rachel, he needs her – and so does Hooper General Hospital. He's determined to help Rachel conquer her fears about nursing, and win her love, but does she have the courage to take them both on?

### THE GREEK SURGEON by Margaret Barker

Sister Demelza Tregarron found herself hoping against hope that Dr Nick Capodistrias and his young son could be the family she'd longed for. In Nick's arms the life she had dreamed about seemed within reach. But when his ex-wife reappeared, Demelza feared she was about to lose those she loved…all over again.

### On sale 5th April 2002

*Available at most branches of WH Smith, Tesco, Martins, Borders, Eason, Sainsbury's and most good paperback bookshops.*

## MILLS & BOON

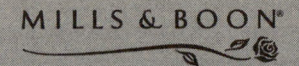

# Medical Romance™

### DOCTOR IN NEED by Margaret O'Neill

Nurse Fiona McFie was damned if she was going to let Tom Cameron walk all over her – and the uneasy attraction that simmered between them made her want to fight him even more. But Tom proved to be a talented doctor and a devoted father, and soon Fiona realised that all she really wanted was to give Tom and his children all the love they could ever need!

### TEMPTING DR TEMPLETON by Judy Campbell

A 'bonding' course certainly isn't Dr Rosie Loveday's idea of fun – until she meets her gorgeous instructor, Dr Andy Templeton. Their mutual sparks of attraction are impossible to ignore, but Rosie is determined to stay single. It's up to Andy to persuade her otherwise and he's got the *perfect* plan!

### MOTHER ON CALL by Jean Evans

Even though it meant juggling single motherhood with a new job, Beth moved to Cornwall so that she could start being a GP again. Then an embarrassing encounter with Sam Armstrong, the new senior partner, marked the beginning of a tense working relationship, made worse by the chemistry they shared. Sooner or later something – or someone – would have to give...

## On sale 5th April 2002

*Available at most branches of WH Smith, Tesco, Martins, Borders, Eason, Sainsbury's and most good paperback bookshops.*

# *Treat yourself this Mother's Day to the ultimate indulgence*

**3 brand new romance novels and a box of chocolates**

# = *only £7.99*

## *Available from 15th February*

*Available at most branches of WH Smith, Tesco, Martins, Borders, Eason, Sainsbury's and most good paperback bookshops.*

0202/91/MB32

# MIRANDA LEE
## Secrets & Sins
### revealed

SEDUCED BY HER BODYGUARD AND STALKED BY A STRANGER...

## *Available from 15th March 2002*

*Available at most branches of WH Smith,
Tesco, Martins, Borders, Eason, Sainsbury's
and most good paperback bookshops.*

**MIRA®**

# Starting Over

*Another chance at love...
Found where least expected*

# PENNY JORDAN

## Published 15th February

*Available at most branches of WH Smith,
Tesco, Martins, Borders, Eason, Sainsbury's
and most good paperback bookshops.*

# FREE
## 2 BOOKS
### AND A SURPRISE GIFT!

We would like to take this opportunity to thank you for reading this Mills & Boon® book by offering you the chance to take TWO more specially selected titles from the Medical Romance™ series absolutely FREE! We're also making this offer to introduce you to the benefits of the Reader Service™—

- ★ FREE home delivery
- ★ FREE monthly Newsletter
- ★ FREE gifts and competitions
- ★ Exclusive Reader Service discount
- ★ Books available before they're in the shops

Accepting these FREE books and gift places you under no obligation to buy; you may cancel at any time, even after receiving your free shipment. Simply complete your details below and return the entire page to the address below. ***You don't even need a stamp!***

**YES!** Please send me 2 free Medical Romance books and a surprise gift. I understand that unless you hear from me, I will receive 4 superb new titles every month for just £2.55 each, postage and packing free. I am under no obligation to purchase any books and may cancel my subscription at any time. The free books and gift will be mine to keep in any case.

M2ZEC

Ms/Mrs/Miss/Mr ..................................................... Initials ............................................
BLOCK CAPITALS PLEASE

Surname ............................................................................................................................

Address .............................................................................................................................

............................................................................................................................

............................................................... Postcode ......................................................

**Send this whole page to:**
**UK: FREEPOST CN81, Croydon, CR9 3WZ**
**EIRE: PO Box 4546, Kilcock, County Kildare (stamp required)**

Offer valid in UK and Eire only and not available to current Reader Service subscribers to this series. We reserve the right to refuse an application and applicants must be aged 18 years or over. Only one application per household. Terms and prices subject to change without notice. Offer expires 30th June 2002. As a result of this application, you may receive offers from other carefully selected companies. If you would prefer not to share in this opportunity please write to The Data Manager at the address above.

Mills & Boon® is a registered trademark owned by Harlequin Mills & Boon Limited.
Medical Romance™ is being used as a trademark.